Dori –

RECKLESS ABANDON

TERI KAY

May your heart always be "Reckless"

Teri Kay

RECKLESS ABANDON

Copyright ©2016 Teri Kay

Reckless Abandon is a work of fiction. All characters, organizations and events portrayed in this novel are either products of the author's imagination or used fictitiously.

First eBook edition: October 2016

Edited By: LJ & CB Creative Images and Services

Cover Design: © Cover to Cover Designs

TABLE OF
CONTENTS

DEDICATION

To my son Ryan Michael
Though we never met, you are my greatest love.
Thank you for being my angel.

PLAYLIST

Just the way you are- Bruno Mars

Wasting All These Tears- Cassadee Pope

Eminem- If I Had

My Darkest Days - Porn Star Dancing

Pink- Glitter In The Air

Zac Brown Band - Highway 20 Ride

Beyoncé - Dance for You

NINE INCH NAILS - "CLOSER"

Van Halen- Hot for Teacher

Miranda Lambert- Scars

Usher- Nice and Slow

Parachute - Kiss Me Slowly

Ariana Grande- Into You

Red Hot Chili Peppers - Dark Necessities

Breaking Benjamin- Angels Fall

Big and Rich- Lovin' Lately

Maroon 5- Harder to Breathe

Sheryl Crow- First Cut is the Deepest

PROLOGUE

1 year ago

Ryann

"What the hell do you mean you're leaving me?" I screamed. "You said this was something you understood."

"I changed my mind," he informed me calmly. "I want kids of my own. That's something you can't give me. I need to find someone who can. I'm sorry."

And with that my husband kissed me on the forehead, placed an envelope on the table and walked out the door. I felt numb. Standing there in our living room, looking around at the memories that we had made in the past ten years, I felt dumbstruck. I heard the powerful engine of his '71 Chevelle pull out of the driveway and roar down the street, and tears burned my eyes. I looked down at our pit bull, Roxy, sitting at my feet. "What the fuck just happened?"

**

I met Lucas McKennan our sophomore year at UNLV. We had a math class together. Math was definitely not my thing, but Lucas seemed to ease through the class. So when he offered to tutor me, who was I to say no. We spent many late nights together cramming for those hideous exams and it wasn't long after that our friendship blossomed into a

3

relationship. I wouldn't it say it was "love at first sight" but I knew there was something special about him. Not to mention, he looked damn hot in his baseball uniform. I spent most of my afternoons staring at Luc's sandy blonde hair, long muscular arms, and perfectly shaped ass while he practiced pitching for the Rebels. More often than not, he'd catch me and give me that panty-melting smile, letting me know what he'd be doing to me later.

The night of graduation, Lucas booked a suite at the Paris Hotel. I walked into a room filled with roses, candles, and the song he always said reminds him of me, "Just the Way You Are" by Bruno Mars, playing in the background.

"I know it's your dream to go to Paris. This is the best I can do right now. Ryann, I want to give you the world. I want us to start a life together. To have a family together. Will you give me the privilege of being my wife?" Again, who was I to say no to my sexy, blonde baseball champ? Lucas had a way of making me feel like a princess. That night my happily ever after was set to begin.

We married six months later in a small ceremony on the Eiffel Tower's Observation Deck at the same place Lucas proposed to me. Since Luc and I were both finishing our education online, we were able to spend the first year of our marriage traveling around the world. We'd been saving for years to be able to take that trip. We put a lock on the Love Bridge in Paris, kissed in the gondolas in Venice, and made passionate love on the beaches of Bali.

Lucas and I treasured every moment we had alone, but

we knew it was time to start our family. Trying for the baby was the fun part...until it wasn't. It became work. Figuring out days, times, and body temperatures became a real pain in the ass. A year later, Lucas and I decided to seek the help of an infertility doctor. After weeks of poking and prodding, and what seemed like an endless amount of blood tests, the doctors determined that I was reason that we weren't getting pregnant.

"Mr. and Mrs. McKennan, my team and I have reviewed the results of your tests. Mr. McKennan, you have some of the strongest swimmers we've seen in a while. What's your secret?"

"Cigarettes and Dr. Pepper," Lucas chuckled. Oh, my God! *Did he really just say that? No, I must have misheard him. Nope, that was my Luc. But wait. If the problem wasn't with Lucas, what did that mean? Holy shit, what was wrong with me?*

"Dr. Ramos, what does that mean about me?" I spoke barely above a whisper.

"Well, Mrs. McKennan we aren't completely sure. Twenty-five percent of all women suffer from some sort of infertility, and of those, another twenty-five percent have an unexplained reason of why they can't have children. All we can suggest at this point is that we continue treatments and keep trying." Ummm, really?

One year later, I got pregnant. Knowing how excited Lucas would be, I wanted to find a special way to tell him. And having no imagination, I of course, browsed through Pinterest. After a bit of scrolling, I found a cookie with the words "Thank you for knocking me up" written in pink and blue icing. Perfect! I decided to make dinner and give him the cookie while we were snuggling on the couch, watching one of those car racing show he loves. When I handed him the box, his eyes almost closed as he smelled the chocolate.

"Cookies! My favorite! What did I do to deserve this special treat?" he asked, as he softly kissed my nose.

"Just open the box, silly," I giggled.

Lucas quickly lifted the lid and read the frosting writing. "Really? We did it?" I nodded. "Holy shit, we're going to be parents!"

A few weeks later, our lives, our relationship, changed forever. Lucas and I were in our usual spot for most Saturday afternoons in the spring. High up in the bleachers watching Rebel baseball. About halfway through the game, I knew something wasn't right. Something was wrong with our baby. Lucas rushed me to the ER, but there was nothing that could be done. We'd lost our baby.

"Well, we'll just keep trying right?" Really? That's all he could say? I'm not sure what I expected, but that wasn't it.

But that's exactly what we did. Every single month. Tracking dates. Eating the right foods. Even only being allowed to fuck in certain positions. Lucas was obsessed with baby-making. All I wanted to do was enjoy my life with my husband. I was beginning to think that having a baby was more important to him than me.

And yet, despite the doctor's thinking the chances for us

were low, I became pregnant once again. Though, much more cautious this time, Lucas and I were convinced that this was our little miracle. We waited until I had made it through the first trimester to make the announcement. But as soon as we hit that milestone, Lucas and I were shouting it from every rooftop in Vegas. He even had them flash it across the marquee at a baseball games. The screen showed one of my ultrasound pictures with the caption: "The future McKennan slugger making their first appearance October 2014". I don't think my love for Lucas could have gotten any deeper that night.

We finally reached that point in the pregnancy when we'd be able to find out if our child was a baseball or softball player. Either way, Lucas and I didn't care as long as our little slugger was healthy.

"How are we today?" Dr. Ramos asked as she entered into the room.

"Anxious! Excited! Ready!" Lucas and I practically said at the same time as the doctor began to squeeze cold jelly all over my tummy.

Dr. Ramos slowly rolled the wand over my abdomen as Lucas and I intently stared at the monitor, trying to see who would be the first to figure out what we were having. But something wasn't right. Something was different this time. The doctor pulled the wand off my small baby bump. "I'm sorry to have to tell you this, Mr. and Mrs. McKennan, but your little girl does not have a heartbeat." My world stopped. Again.

Faintly, I could hear Lucas yelling. It sounded so distant, like he was in a different room. "You're wrong! I want a second *opinion!”*

“I’m sorry, there’s nothing more we can do.”

Everything went dark.

My life, my marriage, my world would never be the same.

**

I stared at that envelope for hours. I knew what was in it. I couldn’t believe it, and I didn’t want to admit, it but I knew it. I had to open it, but I didn’t want to do it alone. I called my best friend, needing a shoulder to lean on.

“Hey, Ryann. I’m doing this stupid class project with Ali. What is it with you teachers and your projects? Can I call you back?” Rose asked.

“Ummm…no. Is there any way you can come over?” I whispered, doing everything I could not to break down on the phone.

“Give me an hour.”

That’s what I loved about my best friend. No questions asked, she was there for me anytime I needed her. We'd been friends since we were twelve, she knew me better than anyone else on the planet. Rose and I have been through everything together. College, wedding, kids, miscarriages, deaths of a parent…but this might be a first for us.

An hour later, Rose arrived with a bottle of Moscato in one hand and a large bag of peanut M&M’s in the other. Like I said, she knew me better than anyone. Even though I'd yet to tell her what's going on, she knew to bring my comfort food. She found me curled up on the couch, using Roxy as a pillow, scrolling through my IPod looking for any sad song I could find.

"What the fuck is going on?" Rose asked.

"You tell me. I can't bring myself to open the envelope Luc left on the table."

Before I could even finish my sentence, Rose was at the table, ripping open the envelope and tearing out its contents. I watched her face as she scanned over the paperwork. Her eyes turned dark and her nostrils flared as the anger took over her face. "What a porchdick!" she yelled.

"What's his reason?" I asked as she started pouring us the largest glasses of wine I've ever seen.

"Irreconcilable differences. Whatever the hell that means." She handed me my wine. I swallowed almost half the glass in the first drink. "Shit, that bad?" she asked.

"He wants kids of his own. I can't give that to him. He doesn't want to foster or adopt. For some reason, after all this time, he decided that having his own kids is more important to him than our marriage. And apparently, I have no say in the matter. His stuff is gone. Obviously divorce papers are drawn up. You know Lucas, when his mind is made up there is no changing it," I cried as the tears began to stream down my face. I really didn't think I had any tears left in me. I gulped down the rest of my wine.

"Oh honey," Rose immediately put her arms around me and let me cry.

"Did he really just ask me for a divorce...?" I mumbled before I drifted off to sleep.

Present Day

Wasting All These Tears

Why the hell was I broke all the time? Oh yeah, I was a teacher. If I'd known ten years ago what I know now, I clearly would have chosen a different path. When I met my ex-husband I wasn't exactly sure what I wanted to do with my life. We spent many late nights laying in each other's arms talking about where our future was headed. From early on in our relationship, I knew that kids were something very important to Lucas. We'd both decided on teaching as a career. I knew I wanted to be the Girl Scout troop leader and Lucas would coach little league. Having a teacher's schedule meant that we could always be home for our kids. We had it all planned out with the white-picket fence, two point five kids, dogs, the whole nine yards. Never did I think at thirty that I would be broke, divorced, and unable to have kids.

As if on cue to get me out of self-pity haze, Ali came crashing through my door.

"Auntie Ry! Are you ready? It's pool day! Let's go swimming." She was about the cutest seven-year-old I'd ever seen. She had long, bouncing, chestnut curls that were the exact color of her big eyes. She was a miniature version of her mother. I was so lucky that Rose and her daughter have been there for me since my divorce. Her family has always been my saving grace.

"In here, baby girl," I yelled from the kitchen. I was filling the cooler up with waters and snacks for our girls' day at the pool.

"Want to help me finish making your favorite? Peanut butter crackers." She immediately ran to the drawer, grabbed her plastic knife and dove into the peanut butter jar. Ali and I have spent time in the kitchen together for as long as I can remember. When she was a baby, I would place her bouncer seat up on the counter and she would just watch me for hours while I baked cupcakes. Our relationship had always been a special one. My divorce was especially hard on her. Just as her and I have that special connection, she also had one with Lucas. He was just beginning to teach her to play tee-ball. One thing about Luc, was that he definitely had a way with kids.

Rose walked in a few minutes later on her cell phone, arguing with her husband again. Work stuff, as usual. I gave her my best stink eye to get off the phone. It was supposed to be our girls' day. She responded by sticking her tongue out at me. I needed reinforcements. I elbowed Ali and she knew just what to do.

I tried not to giggle as Ali dropped her knife and cried out, "Ow! Ow! Ow!" Within seconds, Rose was off the phone and tending to her. Rose treated that little girl like she was made out of glass. Both of us busted out laughing and slapped high fives. "Works every time, Auntie Ry."

"Not funny you two," Rose moaned. Yes. Yes, it was.

Well, to Ali and me it was hysterical. "Are you two brats ready? I need to get my legs out in this beautiful Nevada sun before it gets too hot out there. It's supposed to be 102 degrees by this afternoon." We grabbed the cooler and the pool bag and were off.

Ali jumped in with the neighborhood kids as soon as Rose smothered her in sunscreen. Rose's husband, Jeremy, had insisted that Ali be in swimming lessons as soon as she could walk. Vegas is nothing but swimming pools, and it was a smart thing to make sure your kids were strong swimmers. Ali had recently mentioned wanting to start swimming competitively. At just seven, it was amazing to watch her with the other kids. She loved teaching the little ones how to kick their feet while gliding through the water.

By ten a.m., the pool in my complex had filled up quickly. I snagged one of the cushioned lounge chairs and found the spot where I knew the sun would be most of the day. I grabbed my Kindle and a bottle of water and did my best to settle in for my day of relaxation. I knew I could get lost in the romance of the latest T.J. West novel. Why couldn't real life romance be like that? I would take any of the men of JINKS any day. I thought I had that with Lucas. *Damn it.* It had been almost a year; it was time to stop dwelling on shit from the past.

"So what's up Jeremy's ass now?" I asked Rose trying to change my thoughts.

"Same old shit. Work for him is slow. Construction can be a fickle bitch. Sometimes there's work and sometimes there's not," she shrugged her shoulders. "So while his work is slow, I've picked up some more hours at the club to help bring in some extra money. During the summer months, business really picks up. He's acting all butthurt that I will be spending too much time at work and not enough time with him and Ali. Sometimes he doesn't think things through before he picks a fight."

Rose and Jeremy have been together since they were seventeen years old. The two had this unbelievably deep connection, yet they constantly had these pointless arguments. Rose was stunning; five foot nine with legs for days, stunning dark brown eyes and long tresses to match, a smile that could grab anyone's attention, and the best tits money could buy. Jeremy was tall, ripped with muscles and a southern gentleman. The two of them together were a walking wet dream that melted the panties of both men and women.

"Okay. This week. Next week it's candy and flowers and lovey-dovey time. You two are a never-ending circle." I snickered.

"You wouldn't have it any other way." Rose blew me a kiss and put her ear phones back in, turning her attention back to Ali, and the others playing Marco Polo in the smaller kids' pool.

I glanced around my community's pool and tried to figure out where I fit in the puzzle of relationships. To my left, was the mom brigade. A nice group of women in their thirties and forties, who have their husbands at home barbequing hamburgers, with their flock of kids running all over the place. No matter how hard I tried, I will never be part of that group. To my right, you had the college kids. Young, hard bodied twenty-somethings that are ready to party at moment's notice. Fun to look at, but definitely a scene I happily left years ago. Is there a place for a thirty-year-old divorced, broke teacher?

"Bitch, are you even listening to me?" Rose pushed me and almost knocked me off my chair.

"What the fuck? Sorry, I was daydreaming. What did you say?" I had no idea how long she'd been talking to me.

"Ugh! What do you want to do for your thirtieth birthday? It's coming up next month," Rose asked. Okay, so technically I wasn't thirty, but it was close enough.

"Nothing. I don't care." Rose knew I hated my birthday, but she loved it and I wasn't going to deny her the pleasure of my "Dirty-Thirty" party, as she liked to call it. "You plan. I'll go along with any of your shenanigans," I gave in. I could instantly see her mind working overtime. Oh, dear Lord, what had I just agreed to?

***

What the hell? What time is it? There was a solid banging on my front door. It was the kind of knock you always teased sounded like the cops. Yeah, arrest the boring teacher at...I rolled over to see what time it was...*oh shit*, it was already eleven-thirty. Well, it was *my* birthday.

"Open up! Get your ass out of bed, and answer your door, bitch!" Ah yes, the lovely wake-up call of my best friend. Hooker better have coffee.

"Alright. I'm coming." I rolled out of bed, grabbed a pair of yoga pants that I threw on the floor last night—one of the few perks of living alone—tossed my blonde hair up in a messy bun and looked around for Roxy. I saw my beautiful blue nose pit bull sleeping in her bed in the middle of our small yard, all four of her large paws in the air. You never knew who Rose would bring with her on party nights, and not everyone sees the gentle seventy-five-pound fur baby like I do. That's exactly why I love having her around. Watching people freak the fuck out when she runs up to them and licks their toes is quite amusing.

I slowly made my way to the front door and checked the peephole. Yes, just Rose. And coffee. "Happy thirtieth birthday to my best biotch ever!" she shouted as she pushed her way into my kitchen, with two venti Starbucks and a bag full of muffins. She tossed everything on the counter and rushed back out the door. She came back in with three large boxes in her arms and a large bag draped over her shoulder. "Let the dirty-thirty party begin. It's you and me, babe, for the next few hours, then the glam bitches will get here at three to make us look fierce, and our ride will be here at seven."

"The glam bitches?" I asked, raising one eyebrow at her.

"Yup. Their name not mine. The girls I work with are coming over to give you a head-to-toe make-over for tonight,"

Rose explained.

I looked at myself in the mirror on the dining room wall for a moment. Boring, divorced school teacher. I knew that's the way Rose saw me. Hair in a bun, black rimmed glasses, and shirt buttoned all the way up. Damn, I was a walking cliché. "Am I that bad that I need a whole squad?" I whispered to myself.

"So what's in all the boxes?" I asked, knowing damn well that Rose brought something that I am way too modest to wear out. I've always been the introvert of our group of friends. It's not that I was shy, but I definitely was not the person that liked to have the spotlight on me. Lucas was a light that could shine bright in any room. He was that type of guy that could fit right in no matter where we went. Conversations were easy for him. I was happy just living in his wake.

"Your birthday outfits," Rose said with a sly grin. *Outfits? More than one? What the hell were we doing tonight?*

The next few hours were relaxing. Rose and I caught up on the latest gossip of our friends and family, video-chatted with my grandmother, and laid by the pool for an hour. Our schedules were completely opposite, so our time together these days was precious. Rose was the sister I never had. I wanted to tell her exactly what was going on with my life. I knew she sensed something was off, but being my birthday, she didn't ask. I think she just blew it off as me feeling crappy about turning thirty. And she for sure wasn't going to let that drama-llama takeover, as she so eloquently put it.

New teachers do not make good money. After Uncle Sam, insurance, and retirement all take their cut, I wasn't left with much to live on. What I brought home barely covered my rent and living expenses. Not to mention, my student loans and the damn lawyer fees from my divorce that still plague me every month. Come to find out, when you have been married less than five years, and don't own any property together, you can walk away free and clear. And wouldn't you know that Lucas served me with divorce papers just in time. Being that we only work ten months out of the year, we have those wonderful summer months with no paycheck. For the life of me, I cannot save a dime. Struggling as much as I did was exhausting.

At exactly three o'clock all hell broke loose in my condo. Four girls that work with Rose at *The Cave* came in with every hair, nail, and beauty accessory you could possibly imagine. Some of the devices that they started plugging in I had never even seen before. I thought I was girly, but I was out of my league here. Vanessa (the head glam-bitch) pushed me down in the chair already set up in my oversized bathroom. "Ready to be glamified, teach?" she proudly asked as she started brushing through my long, straight hair. I'd only met Vanessa a few times, but I really did like her.

By the time the girls were done, I seemed like a totally different person. Hair, makeup, and nails all done to the hilt. Rose walked into my room with the first of many birthday shots to find me lost in my reflection. "Honey, what's wrong?"

"Nothing. I promise. I look hot," I paused for a moment as I looked myself up and down. My dress was an absolutely gorgeous sheath lace, navy blue sleeveless mini that fit my ass perfectly. It was a little shorter than I usually wore but at least the girls were covered up. Yet, remembering that Rose used the word outfits still had me nervous. "I just don't look like me, that's all. But, thank you and your friends for all that you've done for me."

"Oh, sweetie. I would never want to change who you are, but did you ever think that maybe it's time to find a new side of you?" Rose hugged me tight, knowing that's exactly what I needed. "The night has just begun. Cheers!" And to that we raised our glasses and let vodka burn down the back of our throats.

The limo arrived at a quarter after seven already full of people. Jeremy and a couple of his work buddies were hitting the mini bar, my brother and his flavor of the month were making out on the back seat, and the few friends that have been by my side since high school were rapidly catching up. As Rose and I climbed in, all I could think was that I was going to make it one kick ass night.

"Hot damn, woman! Looking good," my friend Travis said as he handed me my usual vodka and cranberry. His wife, Ari slapped him on the arm as I kissed her on the cheek and took a seat next to her.

"Thanks." I felt my cheeks turn red. I was totally out of my comfort zone.

"Own it, girl. You looking fucking amazing," Ari said

only loud enough for me to hear.

"Ahem," Rose cleared her throat to get everyone's attention. "Raise your glasses. Here's to having one of the best nights of our lives tonight, to the last of us to have their dirty thirty, and especially to new beginnings."

"And not to forget—it's summer vacation!" I chimed in.

"Cheers!" We all cheered in unison.

**

We pulled up to the Aria right before eight, and I knew the only place we could be going to is Bar Masa for the most amazing sushi in Vegas. As I got out of the limo and we made our way across the casino, I could feel eyes on me from all directions. Or maybe I was just that self-conscious, I wasn't sure. What I did know was that I needed to take Ari's advice and "own this shit" tonight. With a little bit more liquid courage I could maybe make that happen.

When we walked into Bar Masa, they led us to a back room that I didn't know existed, despite the hundreds of times we've eaten there. Must be Rose and her connections. Gotta love Vegas! As we went through the doors, I noticed the green and purple (my favorite colors) motif around the room and balloons everywhere. *Damn her.* We came to the second room and there sat all my family, close friends and co-workers. "Surprise!" They all yelled as they came over to give me hugs like they hadn't seen me ages.

Dinner was absolutely amazing. There's a reason why it was one of the top rated restaurants on the Vegas strip. It was so nice to be able to catch up with my mother before her boyfriend whisked her away on another trip, and also to be able to spend time with my co-workers outside of work; without all their kids running around. I loved their kids to death don't get me wrong, but sometimes the constant reminder is difficult. My thoughts were broken by the sound of Rose tapping her wine glass with a fork.

"I hate to cut this dinner short, but tonight will be an epic night of new and exciting experiences for our birthday girl. We're off to our second destination to start the dirty part of this "dirty-thirty" party. Some of you we will see later and some of you have a great summer," Rose announced. I could see the look of confusion on my teacher friends' faces, wondering what were they being left out of. But if I knew Rose, I didn't need to mix my set of friends anymore tonight.

The same people all piled back in the limo, along with a couple of my cousins that Jeremy's buddies picked up. When we pulled up in the front the Wynn, I instantly got giddy inside. "Oh, please tell me we are going dancing at XS?" I asked Rose. I may be an introvert when it comes to conversations and meeting new people, but on the dance floor I felt free.

"You know it, babe," she gave me a wink as we exited the limo. "Just one quick stop first."

As all my friends went left to the club, Rose grabbed my hand and pulled me off into the other direction. "Where are we going?" I asked.

"Ssshhh, little one," she smiled. "Trust me."

Up the elevators we went. They kept going, and going until we hit the top floor. "Holy shit, you didn't? You can't afford this. Jeremy is going to kill you."

"Like I said before, trust me. I have connections. This place is ours for the night. Enjoy it," Rose boasted.

We walked into the suite and Vanessa's already there waiting for me in the vanity area. "Hey, teach. You ready for outfit number two?"

"What? I'm really liking this one. I'm finally feeling comfortable," I said as I played with the lace hem of the dress.

"Off with the nice family/teacher dress. Time to slip into something sexy to show off those curves, woman. You have a rockin' bod, use it. Let's get you ready to dance the night away," Vanessa demanded as she moved over to the vanity to get me freshened up. She touched up my make-up, re-curled my hair, and tucked me carefully into a skin tight bandage dress. I didn't remember the last time I felt so sexy.

"I'm not sure what I did to deserve all this but thank you guys. I needed it," I said to my friends. I sat there willing myself not to cry. "The past year has been one of the worst of my life, I'm ready to start my thirties off with a bang."

Our next stop was dancing at XS Nightclub. Vanessa's cousin was a bouncer there and was able to hook us up with a VIP booth for the evening. Grey Goose and cranberry were on a constant flow. I lost myself in the rhythm of the music, my body naturally moving with the beats. It was such a Zen feeling to be able to finally let go of the shit that I'd gone through recently and what I was dreading telling my best friend. Or maybe it was the all the alcohol, either way I felt fan-fucking-tastic.

"Hey, beautiful," I froze as I felt arms slide around my waist. "Ready to move on to our final destination? We have something special planned for you." I flipped around to see Vanessa standing quite close. It almost seemed like she was checking me out. *Time to lay off the vodka, Ryann.*

"I'm only beautiful because you made me that way," I teased.

"Keep telling yourself that, sweetheart," Vanessa said as she grabbed my hand and pulled me out of the club.

Porn Star Dancing

I've seen her somewhere before. I can't place it, but I know it will come back to me. I suck at names, but I'm pretty damn good at faces. I'm a professional poker player, it's my job to remember things. I recognized a few of the girls that were dancing around her. Ashlynn, Jade, and Vanessa are dancers here at *The Cave*, and Rose is one of the sexiest bartenders in town. As I watched the blonde beauty move in that dress, my dick twitched in a way it hasn't in a long time. The two-piece number she had on hugged each of her curves in all the right ways. Just enough mesh to let me know that she had some magnificent tits under there. *Porn Star Dancing* started blasting over the speakers and I watched as Ashlynn pulled the blonde on the seat next to her. Jade comes slowly crawling up to them and her eyes went wide. The beauty appeared nervous, but by the way her nipples were piercing through her dress, I could tell she's turned on by all of this.

"Hey, I thought you said Ashlynn wasn't working tonight?" I asked Bree as she dropped off my beer.

"Some kind of private party. Her and Jade are booked for the entire night. Rose and Vanessa took the night off. Birthday party I think," she sighed with a slightly jealous smile.

When I looked back over at the absolutely stunning, obviously over-intoxicated group of women I saw that Jade and Ashlynn had already stripped down to just their G-strings, and were straddling the blonde mystery woman. Damn, that escalated quickly. I knew I shouldn't be watching their private party like some kind of creepy stalker, but I couldn't take my eyes off her. It's not the naked women that are rubbing their breasts all in her face, though they are gorgeous, it's just that blonde is intoxicating. Even from here, I could see the heat in her eyes as she watched the two women dance. The look she gave Jade's body was like an animal wanting to devour its prey. My dick started to ache as it pushed along the seams of my jeans.

Hmmm...there are no guys in their little soiree. Shit, was I really lucky enough to be watching a lesbian stripper party? I laughed to myself.

Judging by the way Nessa hadn't been able to keep her eyes off the blonde beauty, I had to guess that's her girlfriend. I knew Vanessa was in a serious relationship, but I thought she kept that part of her life separate from her club life. What a lucky ass girl. Both of them. I wondered if Vanessa was the type to share. I couldn't help but grin at the naughty images going through my head.

I looked back over at the women, and most of those images were becoming a reality in the booth across the room from me. The blonde mystery woman (I really did need to find out her name) was bending over Vanessa's petite little body, her face buried in those large, completely natural tits. Her ass bounced up and down perfectly to the beat of the music. I noticed that blondie had two butterfly tattoos peeking out of the side of her sheer dress. *Now, I'm really intrigued*. Any woman who can get tatted on her side ribcage is a badass. I needed to know more about her.

"Bree," I called out across the room and waved her over. "Another beer please. Unless Rose over there will make her favorite poker player one of her famous Flaming Doctor Peppers." I flashed my cute, California smile that worked on most girls, pausing when Bree giggled. "And there's an extra twenty bucks in it if you can find out the blonde's name for me over there."

I watched Bree seductively shake her ass all the way over to where Rose was sitting. I knew that she was just trying to get my attention. Bree's cute, but definitely not my type. Too young and way too fake. At nineteen, I'm not sure what is still real on that girl. I heard a rumor that she was trying to get into movies. Bree said something to the group of women that of course I couldn't hear, and all together the six of them turned and stared at me. Tits, ass and all. I don't get embarrassed easily, but damn if there isn't a hole I could run into and hide. I did the next best thing. Held my drink up and offered to buy them a round. Hey, if I am going to be a creepy stalker, I might as well be a gentleman right?

A few minutes later, Rose came over and set down the Stella and shot mixture for my Flaming Doctor Pepper. "Hey handsome," she drawled as she scooched in next to me. Being married to Jeremy for so long, Rose had picked up some of his southern accent. She lit the shot on fire, dropped the beer and I chugged the amazing drink. I could feel the slow burn of the alcohol move all the way down my chest. "If you wanted to know her name all you had to do was come over and ask. It's not like you're some creepy stranger that's been watching us all night." Oh, they noticed. There was a definite slur in Rose's voice. Even drunk she could still make a damn good drink.

Rose kissed me on the forehead, ran her fingers through my short, messy hair, and thanked me for the drink before she started to wiggle herself out my booth. Oh yeah, she was drunk. I gently grabbed her wrist and pulled her back in. "Not so fast there, princess. I paid good money for this drink and now I want the inside scoop." We both laughed, because if I knew Rose, she was going to make me work even harder for information. "How are you all getting home tonight?" She raised a suspicious eyebrow at me like I was up to no good. "Really? Stop thinking the worst. I just want to make sure all you pretty ladies get home safe. Vegas can be a rough town."

"A couple of us are staying at the Wynn and the rest are being taken home in the limo," Rose answered.

"How about this? When you ladies are ready to walk back to your hotel, let me be your escort in exchange for the blonde beauty's name, deal?" I asked.

"Deal."

For the next hour, I watched the stunning group of strippers, lesbians, and a bartender continue to drink, party, and take more clothes off. All but the blonde beauty. Her clothes seemed to stay perfectly in place. Her skirt may have been lifted up a few times, but never enough to allow me to see that luscious round ass she was hiding up underneath there. We made eye contact a few times and each time I caught her looking at me, she would quickly turn away. Fuck, she was beautiful.

When they brought the cake out, I realized it was blondie's thirtieth birthday party. It was a giant mound cake that was a very accurate depiction of tits and ass. It was long past closing time, but for a VIP party *The Cave* would stay open any hours. And all of these women were our VIPs. Me, being their designated chaperone, was the lucky SOB who got to stay and watch. Not wanting to be the only guy amidst this group of beautiful, drunk women I kept my distance during the party. Something told me there was more than meets the eye with those ladies.

By the end of the night, or the early morning, however you wanted to look at it, I wasn't sure I was as lucky as I thought. I walked out from taking a piss and looked around the room. Bree's full red lips were sucking the frosting off Jade's large nipples. *Sexy? Hell yes!* But probably not something you should be doing at work. Vanessa and Ashlynn were snuggled up together in a dark corner. Oh fuck, yes. My blonde beauty wasn't Vanessa's girlfriend. Oh, but shit, Ash is? Wow. Again not something you wanted to do at work. But where was my blonde beauty? Fuck, I still needed to learn her name. I looked around and saw her laying across a table looking like she's going to be sick. Time to get these ladies home.

"Alright ladies," I stood up and shouted in the middle of the room. "Time to wrap it up." I immediately go to the blonde beauty and picked her up off the table and carried her to the couch in the back office. As she wrapped her arms around my neck, I smelled her hair. Coconut. Something so California beachy about that. I definitely needed to put that in my memory bank. The last thing I wanted to do was put her down, but I had a room full of drunk, frosting covered strippers that I needed to deal with.

I shuffled the girls into the limo, and despite their drunk pleas to join them, I closed the door and sent them on their way. What warm-blooded, straight male really shuts the door and ignores the invite of four drunk strippers? A smart one that's who. I learned my lesson with strippers a long time ago. I bee-lined back into the office to see Rose and the mystery woman snuggled up on the couch together. "Fucking sexy." But as sexy as Rose was, her husband was a big dude. Not a line I would ever cross in the first place. I'd be asking Jeremy more about Rose's friend though.

"Let's go, my beauties," I whispered as I gently shook Rose awake and scooped her friend into my arms. Damn, her body felt good next to mine. She nuzzled her face into my neck, looked up at me with big brown eyes and whispered, "You're really cute," and fell right back to sleep. I led them out of the club, heading for my truck.

"Umm...we can ssswalk," Rose spit out as she tripped over the edge of the walkway. "Okay, maybe not."

The Wynn was only two blocks away, but Vegas at four in the morning could be a sketchy place, even for a bigger guy like me. I pulled into valet and told the kid to hold it up front and that I was just dropping the ladies off. "Yes sir, Mr. Sims." It was still a kick being recognized here and there. Being semi-famous in Las Vegas was a definite perk.

I got the girls up to their suite safely, and Rose had started to sober up enough to take over babysitting duties. I laid the sleeping, snoring angel down on her oversized bed and had to resist the urge to crawl in bed with her and hold that beautiful body against mine. I've never even spoken to this girl and yet I couldn't wait to see that smile again. I brushed a piece of hair that fell across her nose off her face and gently tucked it behind her ear. Something about her was different.

"Thank you for making sure we all got home safe tonight, Nathan," Rose said loudly next to me, watching her friend. Again, not trying to look like a creepy stalker, I reluctantly pulled my eyes away to meet Rose's.

"Shh! don't wake her up," I whispered. "Looks like she's had a long night."

"Uh. No. Watch this!" Rose then proceeded to jump up and down on the bed yelling, "Wake up! Wake up!" Okay, maybe she wasn't that sober yet. Blondie didn't move a muscle. The whole scene was actually quite humorous.

"Alright. On that note, I'm outta here. Go to bed, Rose!" I ordered and started to let myself out.

"Wait!" Rose shouted. Well if she didn't wake Sleeping Beauty over there, she'll at least piss off the neighbors. "Thought you wanted to know her name?"

Fuck, how could I forget that? "Of course I do." I flipped around to see Rose standing right in front of me.

"Vaughn. Vaughn Haley," she chuckled and closed the door behind me.

On the drive back to my place, I couldn't help but to keep from running her name through my head. Vaughn Haley. Something unique and strangely familiar about that name. She didn't have a ring on her finger so that was a good thing. I was happy as fuck to find out she wasn't Vanessa's girlfriend. I hadn't seen her around the club before so I didn't think she was a dancer. "Vaughn Haley," I repeated out loud. "Fuck that does sound like a stripper name." I really hoped she wasn't one of the girls. Dating strippers was one of my hard limits.

As I pulled into my driveway, my cell phone alarm started going off. "Awesome. Time to wake up and I haven't even gone to bed yet." Spending the evening meeting Vaughn, even though we never actually spoke, may just have been worth feeling like shit all day.

Once inside, I grabbed an energy drink from the fridge. Yeah, that stuff's bad for me but it still tastes better than coffee. Figuring out how much time I had before I needed to leave for the airport, I decided to go on a quick run to clear my head from the previous night's festivities. My ten-year-old English bulldog, Cheech, was sprawled out on my loveseat, snoring away. I got crap for his name every time I introduced him to someone new, but that dog has been with me since I was a college stoner math whiz. Those days were long behind me, for the most part, but the old beast was still with me.

By the time I got home from my run, I had just enough time to enjoy a hot shower, grab my stuff and hit the road. Again. Oh, the life of a professional poker player. Most of what I did is here in Las Vegas, but there are some high dollar tournaments all over the world. This week it was Atlantic City, New Jersey.

During my shower, I couldn't help but think about Vaughn. She was one of the most beautiful women I'd ever seen. There was something more innocent about her than most of the girls I'd met, especially the ones that party all night with strippers.

I thought about the way she danced with her face pressed into Vanessa's full chest and my dick instantly went hard. There was no way I could be on a plane for the next five hours with a raging hard-on. Her perfect tits bouncing up and down in that nearly see-through dress swam before my vision as I started to run my hand up and down my shaft. It wasn't going to take me long to cum. My dick had been hard since the moment I laid eyes on Vaughn earlier that evening. I felt my balls tighten and they were quickly ready to explode. I closed my eyes and saw her sweet, sexy smile as I carried her to my truck. That right there, that image, sent me right over the edge. My cum ran over my fist as I let the memory of her beauty take over my release.

"Time to go make some money, baby," I said as I got myself out of the shower and ready to leave.

Glitter in the Air

When I woke up, I could already feel the bright morning sunshine burning my legs. Damn the Nevada summer heat had already arrived. As soon as I sat up, the entire room started spinning like I was on one of those tea cup rides at an amusement park. I gripped the edge of the bed to prevent myself from falling down. "Where the hell am I?" I whispered as I surveyed the room around me. I vaguely remembered some cute guy with tattoos for days carrying me to bed. Oh shit, did I hook up with up some random guy last night? I heard breathing behind me. I was scared to death to turn around; to see who was in bed with me. Rose wouldn't let me do that, would she? I sat there for a minute and tried to remember the night before.

"Oh good, you're up," Rose said as she dug her foot into my back. "Go get us Starbucks. It's your turn," she groaned.

Oh, thank God it was Rose in my bed. "Um, nope it's actually your turn," I plopped down on the pillow next to her. "What the hell happened last night? Thanks by the way, I had an amazing time. Well what I can remember. And thanks for sending the guys home before we went to *The Cave*. It was so much easier to relax."

"I got the coffee yesterday. And last night was a fricken' blast. And I knew it would be for you. What happened, you ask? Check Instagram under the name, Vaughn Haley," Rose said coyly.

"Yesterday was my birthday so those coffees don't count. See, your turn. And really? Public pictures? You know how I feel about that!" I was getting slightly pissed off. "And who the hell is Vaughn Haley? Is she one of the strippers? I told you I don't like that crap!" I yelled.

Rose gave me the—I'm not taking any more of your crap—look. "Alright, cool your shit. Go grab your phone and look her up. I'll call room service. You need coffee and some damn chill pills."

I rolled over and grabbed my phone off the nightstand, brought up the app and typed in Vaughn Haley. There was a couple of people with that name. Wait, why did one have my face? Obviously that's the profile I was looking for. I clicked on her name. This chick only has two followers. What's the point in even having an Instagram with only two followers? I started scrolling through all the pictures and they were all of me from last night. What the hell was going on? "Rose, could you come in here please? And the coffee better be here!" I yelled to her.

She came walking in, luckily with coffee in hand. "I can explain. The story is actually kind of funny," she laughed, handing me some aspirin as well.

"Oh it better be. And who is IGotTheNuts21? And why is he the only other person besides you who likes this profile?" I asked.

Between the Instagram photos, Facebook tags, and what little was left of our memory, Rose and I pieced together most of the night. "I can't believe that Nathan's Instagram name is IGotTheNuts. I never pictured him as gay," Rose scrunched her nose, looking slightly puzzled.

"Why the hell would you think he was gay? Because his screen name has the word nuts in it? Oh, you can't be that dumb," I replied as I picked up a pillow and tossed it at her. "You said he's a poker player right?" She nodded. "Okay, dingbat, Nuts is a poker term meaning having the best possible hand at any given time. I really am going to miss you."

"Well that makes more sense. Wait, what? Miss me? Where are you going? What's going on with you? I knew there was something you weren't telling me," Rose barked, irritated.

I crawled back into the bed next to her like we've been doing since we were teenagers. "I'm moving back to California with my mom and her boyfriend at the end of the month." My breath hitched as I finally revealed the truth. "I love my mother, but living with her and Stuart is not how I wanted to start off my thirties. But I'm broke, Rose. Like straight up, barely squeaking by paycheck to paycheck broke."

My mother met Stuart a few years back on a senior's single cruise to Mexico, and according to her it was love at first sight. He's been good for her, and makes her happy.

When my mom's happy and off traveling with Stuart, she stays off my back. She loved Lucas, according to her he was the best thing that had ever happened to me. Arguments between us often led to her blaming me for our divorce. Needless to say, our relationship has been rocky over the past year. So having to live with her was not something that even remotely appealed to me. And to make matters worse, Stuart is a self-proclaimed nudist. I unexpectedly figured that out when he jumped off the couch last Thanksgiving when I came to visit them for the first time. Let's just say he was excited when his team scored a touchdown.

"Why haven't you said anything?" she asked. I knew she wanted to help, there was nothing she could do.

"There's nothing you could have done to help. Since the divorce, it's been a struggle to make ends meet. I need a place that allows me to have Roxy, so I had to stay at the condo. New teachers don't make the best money, so I'm just surviving. I want to live not just survive," I explained as I blankly stared out the window. The last thing I wanted to do to was live with my mother in Northern California. I loved this town. Las Vegas became my home when Rose and I moved away from the small town we were raised in. When I got accepted to the University of Las Vegas, she came to Nevada with me and went to Bartending School. It's the reason I didn't leave after my divorce. But I'd run out of options.

We sat there in silence together for a few minutes. I knew Rose was trying to figure out ways for me to stay. "I've already gone through every scenario. Going back home for a while is my only option," I explained.

"Come work at *The Cave*!" Rose blurted out.

"And do what?" I asked with my typical smart ass tone. "You know they don't need another bartender. I'm an awful server. Remember Denny's 2006? Four broken plates, a sprained ankle, and some guy ended up with marinara burns. The only other thing at *The Cave* is dancing."

"Well…" she gave me a contemplative look. "Those girls make damn good money. I'd do it if it wasn't for Ali. And Jeremy, I guess."

"Are you serious? Last night I had an issue with wearing a dress that was too short or showed too much cleavage in front of my friends. And now you suggest I shake my naked lady bits in front of strangers. Obviously you're still drunk!" I huffed and stormed out of the room, slamming the bathroom door. Rose knew me well enough to not to say shit to me in that moment. I poked my head out the door. "AND WHAT IF ONE OF MY STUDENTS SAW ME?" I screamed at her.

Rose literally spit her coffee out all over the bed. "You teach fucking kindergarten!" she screamed right back at me.

I loved my best friend, but at the moment, I absolutely hated her. She knew I couldn't dance at *The Cave*. I couldn't, could I? No, there's no way in hell I could ever strip. I'm a kindergarten teacher for goodness sake.

I lived for the oversized tubs in hotel suite bathrooms. It's just what I needed before I had to go back to reality. One day, when I bought a house of my own, I was going to make sure it had the most magnificent tub. I let the hottest water I could handle fill the tub and added in a few drops of coconut scented bubble bath. I lit the candle that was on the counter, and powered on my Ipod to my escape playlist. Pink's *Glitter in the Air* played through the speakers. I carefully stepped in and let my body sink down until I was almost neck deep in the water. The lyrics completely filled my mind as tears slowly started falling down my face.

"Hey, Ryann," Rose softly knocked on the door. "Can I come in, honey? Can we talk?"

"Yeah, it's open." I wiped my eyes. I really didn't need Rose to see me crying. "What's up?"

"Look the last thing in the world I want to do is make you upset, but the thought of losing you is the worst thing that could happen to me. We've never lived more than fifteen minutes apart from each other since middle school. The thought of you being over ten hours away kills me. Maybe I'm being selfish. I know teaching is your passion, but maybe you could make dancing your job for a while? At least until you can get a handle on your finances. The girls at *The Cave* make anywhere from five to seven hundred a night. You could dance through summer vacation and make plenty of money to get caught up and put some away for the school year." Rose looked at me like she had the answers to all my problems wrapped up in one little ball.

"Don't you think I've thought about all of this?" The hurt I was feeling inside at the thought of leaving my best friend caused my tone to come out sharper than I intended. "Do you realize the consequences if I get caught? I'd lose my teaching credential. Everything I've worked so hard for. Not to mention I'm not one for the spotlight. You know how shy I am. There's no way I could parade around naked in the club."

"First of all, it's topless, not nude," Rose retorted. "Second, you know Vanessa could completely change your appearance so no one will recognize you. And last, I'd bet you'd be shocked to find out what most of these women do during the day, so stop looking down your damn nose on us. We have an hour until check out." With that, Rose stood up and walked out, leaving me alone with just my tears.

**

It's been four days since Jeremy picked Rose and I up at the Aria after our fight, and she had yet to call me. Her stubborn streak was good. Better than mine, that's for sure. I hated not talking to her. But with the silence, I had nothing but time to think. Think about if I could really have the confidence do what she suggested. If I could really live with my mother and Stu (Hmm. Confidence booster right there). Too often I found myself thinking about Mr. Nuts. Each time I looked at the Vaughn Haley Instagram, I noticed him. Nathaniel was only in the background of all the pictures. He never joined the party, leaving me to wonder why.

At nine-thirty that night, I drove to *The Cave* to finally talk to Rose. Thursday's are usually her slow nights so we should have some time. I snuck in and her back was to the door. She didn't see me. The place was packed. Rose told me things usually picked up during the summer months, but damn this was crazy.

"Hey, baby, can I have an Angel's Tit?" I asked in my best manly voice.

"Sorry, we don't serve perverts here," she retorted as she turned around and chuckled.

"Ouch. That one hurt," I pretended like I was shot in the chest. "But you gotta admit that's a pretty good one!"

"You have to stop Googling dirty drinks. What's up? I'm working and we're a little busy. Some country festival bullshit," she yelled over a group of rowdy cowboys.

"I was hoping we could get a chance to talk about things," I told her.

"Well can we do that at home, please?" Rose asked.

"I can't apply for a summer job from home," I smiled.

"Good thing I have an in with the management. Let's go talk to Vanessa." Rose grabbed me by the wrist and dragged me into Vanessa's office.

***

Rose and the girls took me shopping the next morning for everything I needed. Apparently, the club doesn't provide your outfits. And now that I thought about it, that's probably a good thing. Ewww, gross. I would not want to share things with some of the other girls. There's a plethora of costume, lingerie, and sex shops in Las Vegas to help me create the exact persona I wanted to become each night. Outfits were needed for floor and lap dances, the stage performances, catering to the fantasies of certain clients, and for the different theme nights when the club put on a party and the girls dressed similar. And I needed at least three outfits for each night, according to Jade. Well, there goes my emergency credit card. But I guess somewhere in this crazy world, stripper heels are considered an emergency.

At lunch, Vanessa and Ashlynn gave me the run-down of how a typical night at the club worked. I had no idea that you actually had to pay the club to be able to dance there. It's like their cut. "The harder you hustle, the more dollars in your G-string," Ashlynn said to me. Made sense. "Just a few simple rules to live by. One: Only participate in what makes *you* comfortable. Don't let anyone make you do something you don't feel comfortable with. Two: Don't date the clients. It always turns out messy," she chuckled. "Okay. I didn't mean for it to sound like that. And three: The most important rule, have fun. Loosen up with a few drinks if you need to, but don't get drunk. Sloppy strippers are no bueno. I watched a girl walk right off stage once." Ashlynn had a sense of humor that could make anyone laugh.

"Seems easy enough," I replied with a nervous smile. The rest of our lunch went by smoothly. We talked about the policies and the rules at *The Cave*. The differences between pole, floor and stage dances and how with each you created a different character. Each of the girls at the club had a signature dance. I was going to need to figure out mine and soon. "So when will they teach me the dances?" I questioned.

"Oh girl, no one teaches you," Bree informed me with

her cute southern drawl. "Nope. You're on your own to figure out your moves."

Vanessa must have sensed my nervousness, and sought to put me at ease. "Ready for your make-over?" she asked.

I shrugged my shoulders. "I guess."

"Ladies, we'll see you later. I'll bring Ry with me tonight and then I think I we need an emergency girl's night after work. I'll text you all the details." Vanessa grabbed me by the wrist and yanked me out of the restaurant.

The drive to Vanessa's place was quiet. The thought of whether or not I had the confidence do this kept running through my mind. I was honestly scared to death. What no one knew, not even Rose, was that I could dance. And I was pretty damn good too. After Lucas left me, I needed to find something to make me feel like a woman again, something to make me feel sexy. I found a pole fitness Groupon and figured why the hell not. I became addicted. So instead of the gym, I took classes twice a week in private or in Jewel's dance studio. I was a sexy beast, but this had yet to be tested in front of others. It was my dirty little secret.

Vanessa had a small place on the outskirts of Las Vegas. Perfect for her and her cat, Hairball. The extra room was set up as a complete dressing room. I was undeniably jealous.

"So we have a good five hours until we have to leave for work. Let's figure you out," Vanessa said as she started pouring us a glass of wine. Vanessa was the entertainment manager for the club. She was more like a den mother to the girls at *The Cave* than a boss. She was in charge of helping the girls get settled in and to find their way, so to speak.

We walked back and sat in front of the vanity mirror in the dressing room. "I'm scared, Nes. I'm older than most of the girls at the club. What if I get rejected because they think I'm too old? What if I fall flat on my face? What if someone recognizes me?" I rambled on.

"Rose was right. You do worry too much," she answered as she got up and stood behind me. "One thing at a time. First, I'm eight years older than you, girl. I don't get rejected. It's all in your attitude. You have a smoking hot body. Get up. Go stand in front of the mirror.

"What?" I questioned. "Why?"

"Do it," she demanded. Even though Vanessa is only five foot three and I stood a good five inches over her, I wouldn't dare argue with her. "Strip. Take it all off, Ryann." I took off my clothes and stood there looking at myself in the mirror. I felt exposed and tried to cover myself up. Vanessa pulled my hands down. I've always kept myself in good shape, but I've been less confident in myself as a woman since the divorce, even with the classes. The feeling that I was somehow broken, not good enough, has been slowly dragging me down as my situation got worse and worse. "If you can't feel comfortable being naked in front of me, how can you do it in front of hundreds of men and women?" she asked softly.

"Women?" I shyly repeated.

"Yes, honey. It's Vegas. They all show up. Do you know

what I see in front of me?" I shook my head. "A striking woman who will soon gain back her confidence this summer. You're tall, with amazingly strong legs. You have these cute perky tits, just like mine," she laughed as she grabbed her own boobs and jiggled them around. "Not saggy from those pesky kids sucking on them for years. And obviously you do some squats, because this ass is like two perfectly shaped globes. You want to look different, I can make that happen and I understand your reasons, teach. But embrace this body you have. Not all of us are as blessed as you." I put on one of the silk robes that she handed me.

"Do you really think I can do this, Vanessa?" I searched her face for the reassurance I needed.

"This might sound weird, but hear me out. You teach kindergarten, right? So what's your day really about? Putting on a show to keep the attention of a group five-year-olds. Essentially, throughout the day you become many different characters to teach them what they need to know. The purpose at a strip club quite similar. Most of our customers are overgrown drunk boys anyways. Become the character, but rather than teach them, take their money. The best advice I can give you is listen to your customer. They're paying you. Create their fantasy." She finished her speech and I started to feel a little more confident in the situation.

"Alright. Let's make me over," I said to her with a cautious grin.

Dance for You

It felt so good to be home. I took a long swig off my beer, my eyes glued to the latest MMA fight that I missed, while playing catch with my pup. I loved what I do, but all the traveling begins to wear on you. I spent the last week in Atlantic City playing in a week long Texas Hold'em tournament. I guess I couldn't complain too much, I made over $122,000 for five days of "work".

Poker is something that requires one's complete attention to be successful. All week, I couldn't help but let my mind wander to thoughts of Vaughn. That blonde hair, her dark brown eyes, her perfect curves. It really didn't help my game. That girl had quickly captured my attention. I wanted to call Rose and ask about her, but as far as anyone knew, I was just a club regular. Even though I've hung out with Jeremy and Rose casually outside of *The Cave,* I wasn't ready to share my actual involvement in the establishment. And a customer calling a bartender for her drunk friend's number may not go over too well. I guess I could have sent Vaughn a direct message on Instagram, but after she didn't follow me back I again didn't want to turn into that creepy dude in the background. Even though that's exactly what I was.

"Well, shit. That fight lasted less than fifteen minutes.

Now what?" Eight-fifteen on a Saturday night and I had not a damn thing to do. You would think that living in Vegas I would never run out of things to keep me busy. But the party lifestyle just wasn't me. I liked to drink, but for the most part, I was pretty mellow. Most of my friends were still in California or are just poker buddies. And when you live your life in casinos, they're the last place you want to go on your time off. But there's no way I was sitting at home by myself my first night back in town.

I grabbed my iPhone and hit the Facetime App. I scrolled through my list of contacts until I found her name. I hit call. She picked up within two rings.

"Hey, beautiful." I smiled as her face appeared on my screen. Those eyes got me every time.

"Hi," she said sadly, and gave me that cute pout.

"What's wrong, baby girl? Where's that smile that makes me so happy?" I asked.

"It's in Las Vegas," she replied with that nine-year-old attitude I had grown to love so much.

"What does that mean?"

"I miss you, Daddy," she whined. "It's almost summer break and I really want to come and visit."

"I miss you too, J-Ella Bean. That's why I'm calling. Talk to your mom. Figure out the days when you can come and spend a couple weeks with me. I'll text you both the few days I will be gone this summer for tournaments, but you can always stay with your aunt and cousin during that time," I told her. We continued to talk for a few more minutes about all the end of year things going on at school and my latest trip. We blew each other our special father/daughter kiss and ended our chat. The day I moved away from Ella was the worst day of my life, but to continue my career, I needed to be in Las Vegas. I hated not being able to tuck her in each night, so video chats were our next best thing. She said she understood but it still broke my heart.

Well, that was a half an hour off my nothing to do Saturday night. Might as well shower and go hit up *The Cave*, have a few good drinks and maybe a lap dance or two. I may not be into dating strippers, but Ashlynn is that type of girl that can make your body forget the stresses of traveling and sitting on uncomfortable poker table chairs for five days.

I decided to ride my Harley to the club. Saturday night traffic in Vegas could be a bitch, and my bike allowed me to get around much quicker. I loved the free feeling of being able to roar up the downtown strip. The parking lot to *The Cave* was packed. Typical for a weekend night. I pulled up around back and went directly into Damon's office.

"Hey, bud," I greeted him as I entered the club. "How's it going?" I dropped down in the chair in front of his desk.

"Nuts! Good to see you, buddy," he shouted. "How was the tournament? Better yet, how were the hotties of Atlantic City?"

"You're lucky I like you, asshole." I gave him a dirty look. He's the only person that can still get away with calling me nuts. I met Damon White at UCLA our freshman year. He had just started an underground poker tournament each month in the dorms. I got the nickname nuts a few years later in one of the weekend tournaments. It didn't seem to matter which table I was at that night; I was constantly being dealt the best hands. After that night, I began to take my poker playing a little more seriously. "It was good. Fourth place. Dude, it's Jersey. There are no hotties. How's business?"

"Boomin' buddy! Boomin'!" He smiled.

"That's what I like to hear. I'll catch up with you later. I need one of Rose's Flaming Doctor Peppers," I told him as I walked out. Nobody ever thinks much of me coming and going from the back because Damon and I have been best friends since college. *The Cave* was even more crowded tonight than a usual Saturday. These music festivals really upped the number of people in here. The husband's send their wives to the concerts and they come and hang out here for the night. Smart if you asked me. I made my way through the crowd to the main bar to grab a drink from my favorite bartender.

"Hey, handsome," she said as she dropped the shot into the beer. She must have seen me coming from the back. "I have a break in twenty minutes. I'll meet you upstairs."

I nodded and headed toward the VIP lounge. I loved the view that the corner booth gave me. I was able to see the entire stage, two of the three bars, and the front door. I believed seeing who was coming and going in the club was important. Being a professional gambler, I never liked to be blindsided. I only put myself in positions where I held the cards.

Ashlynn came over with my usual beer and Jack Daniel's shot. "Hey, stranger. Haven't seen you in a few weeks." She bent over to put the drink down on my table and I could see directly down the small, pink camisole thing she was wearing. Her perky, petite tits were actually looking quite luscious. Ashlynn had natural strawberry blonde hair and soft, pale skin. The pink in her top almost perfectly matched her erect, little nipples. She crawled in the booth behind me, sat on top of one the seats and started rubbing my shoulders.

Shit, she didn't remember last weekend. Ashlynn was pretty well shit-faced drunk when I put her in the limo with the other girls. Should I say something? I let out a moan as she rubbed my neck. The last thing I wanted was for things to become awkward between Ash and I. She's been my girl for the last few months, and she's never mentioned being in a relationship with Vanessa. "Tournaments have been keeping me busy," was all I could think of saying. She moved down the bench next to me and pulled my legs over her body. Ash began rubbing my quads in a way that made my whole body shake. "How's school?" I managed to spit out. My eyes practically rolled back in my head. Damn the woman had magic hands.

"Good. Hard. I didn't realize how much medical terminology there is in massage therapy. But I'm enjoying what I do and the clients I get to practice on," she answered with a wink.

"Well I love being your massage dummy, Ash." The D.J. played the siren which told all the stage performers of the night that they had five minutes until their next number.

Ashlynn hopped up. "That's my cue, babe. It's Beyoncé night." She bounced down the stairs and disappeared through the back curtain. I enjoyed watching the group dances that are performed at the club. We definitely had some of the sexiest woman in Vegas. Within minutes, Beyoncé's *Dance for You* was playing throughout the club and most of the dancers were on the stage. It's a slower song and the girls used it to bring those "totally unsuspecting bachelor's" up on stage and gave them the lap dance of their life before they ran off and got married. I watched as Jade and Ashlynn worked together and scared the piss out of a young kid. The poor guy looked like he just came straight off a farm in Iowa. Jade was standing behind him, having him look up as she shook her tits right over his face. Ashlynn was doing this reverse cowgirl kind of thing, grinding her ass in the guy's lap. By the time the song was over, it wouldn't have surprised me if farm boy down there didn't bust a nut in his pants.

It's long past twenty minutes and Rose had still not come up to talk to me. The bars would usually clear out a bit when there were group numbers on the stage. I spotted her talking to a hot new redhead. She was sitting on one of the tall stools legs crossed, you could almost see the defined muscles in her legs. Definitely a dancer's legs. Her back was bare, except for a small tattoo that I couldn't make out from my position. Her natural tan practically glowed under the low club lighting. Screw watching from up here. Time for another

FDP.

As I made it to the bottom of the stairs, the little red headed vixen walked away with Vanessa. Damn. Next time. I made my way over and occupied the stool she was sitting in. There was a lingering scent of coconut in the air. Immediately, my dick jerked in my shorts. I looked around for my blonde beauty but no such luck. Probably just a coincidence. I mean coconut had to be a popular scent among the ladies during the summer. I watched the girls on stage as Rose finished up with other customers.

"Hey, Nathan. Sorry we're busy tonight. I just wanted to say thanks for making sure my girlfriend and I got back to our hotel safely last weekend. Jeremy also says thanks. He says hit him up for a workout sesh," Rose shouted over the music as she poured my drink.

I didn't even notice that Vanessa and Vixen returned to the bar while I was finishing my shot. "Hey, champ," Vanessa bumped me with her hip. "Meet my newest summer dancer..." I glanced over to my right and saw her standing there. Vanessa ceased to exist for me after that.

I would have recognized those dark eyes anywhere. They'd invaded my dreams for the past week. Why was my blonde beauty now this red headed vixen? Was this her? Or was I just that exhausted that I was thinking that any girl that smells like coconut was her? She turned to grab a drink off the bar, and I saw them; the two butterfly tattoos that decorated her side. She shook my hand, "I'm sorry, I missed your name," I questioned.

"Vaughn. Pleased to meet you, Mr. Sims," she said demurely.

No. Fucking. Way. Vaughn. My blonde beauty was a stripper.

**

"I'm going to lose it all, man. Everything I worked so hard for is going to shit and all I can do is admit that you were fucking right," Damon said as he put his head in his hands. His wife left him three months ago when she decided that being married just wasn't for her. I warned him not to marry Isabell. There was always something about her I didn't trust. Fake, little gold digger from Miami. I saw that one coming a mile away, and ran. Damon was convinced Isabell was his soulmate and married her way too quickly. Within a year they bought a house, two new high end cars, and he even put her name on the deed to his fucking club. I had been hearing the gossip around town about her only being in it for the money. Vegas may be a big town, but people here love to run their mouths. Especially strippers. Rumor had it, Isabell only planned to stay long enough to take half and then she was out of there. I hated to say I told you so, but I called it on day one. I'm a poker player. I could usually see when people were bluffing. Damon doesn't have an ounce of card shark in him, and when it came to Isabell he only saw her with his dick rather than his eyes.

"Dude, we will figure it out. We always do. Give me a week. I may have a solution," I told him as we watched the girls dance on stage. Life may suck at times, especially when your

lady walked out on you and took half of everything, but having a huge set of tits bouncing up and down in front of you, can certainly make you forget for a while. As for me, I might just reap the benefits of my friend's misery. The tits were just a perk. Yeah, I'm a selfish bastard sometimes.

A week later, I invited Damon, his lawyer and my financial advisor to lunch. "Gentlemen, I have a business plan that may get us all what we want in this situation. My advisor and I have been looking for different ways to invest my poker winnings, something where I can be a silent partner. And all I know is poker and women. Everything else is left up to Damon."

"Man, really? I know my way around the ladies," Damon laughed.

"Dude, if you did, none of us would be here right now. Now, back to business. In front of you is a business plan for The Cave, what could be Vegas' hottest new strip club and bar. The club you have now, Damon, is not the club you dreamed of having. We can sell it. Give Isabell half of the money and get the hell away from her. I've found the prime location two blocks from the Aria that's twice the size of what you have now," I explained.

"Sounds great man, but the half I get from the club won't be able to buy and create The Cave. Nice idea though," Damon voice held a hint of defeat.

"And that's where I come in. I need something to invest in. I'll be a silent partner. The plan we've drawn up say the profits are one hundred percent yours until you're free and clear from Isabitch." The whole table chuckled. "Once you pay

me back, we'll split the profits seventy-five and twenty-five percent. If that works for you. I'm serious about being a silent partner, besides on paper this is your club. I just request my own VIP booth," I laughed as my friend and his lawyer were going over the paperwork.

With that, The Cave was born. Because this was an investment that I would be spending a great amount of time at, I wanted it to be a place where I could come and just chill out. We wanted The Cave to be different than the other strip clubs in Vegas. We definitely had the room, with the building being one of the largest three stories in the area. Damon and I came up with the idea that every man needed his cave, and designed rooms and bars with a particular theme in mind. Within six months, we were up and running; within a year we had made the Las Vegas top ten list of best strip clubs. We were obviously on the right track. I had definitely made the right investment with my winnings, despite my advisors' hesitations.

After watching the dismay of so many relationships of the people around me, a girlfriend was not something that I wished to pursue. I was married to the game of poker. Keeping me up late, taking all my money, and making my back hurt like a bitch. Yeah, the game of poker was all the woman I needed. Anything else was just a distraction to my success. But of course, like any other red-blooded man I got horny and needed the feel of a soft woman underneath my body. Surprisingly, there are poker groupies. Women thinking they can fuck their way into your heart and grab a piece of your winnings. Yeah, I may be one of the younger players on the tour, but I was not the naive pup most of these cougars think they were getting *their claws into. My life became the epitome of wham, bam, thank you, ma'am.*

I had been in Australia for the past month playing in the Down Under Hold 'em tournament. After being on a plane for the past seventeen hours I was ready to crawl into my booth at The Cave with Vanessa and forget the bad luck streak my trip ended on. Vanessa's been with us at The Cave since it opened and she and I had developed a genuine bond. I had yet to fuck her, but definitely thought about how nice her pussy would feel wrapped around my cock. Her petite frame, huge tits that were all her own, and ass that would keep any man following her around had made my dick hard quite a few times. At first, Vanessa was just doing the job I paid her to do by listening to me, but over the past year we had genuinely become friends.

"Hey, champ," she said as she seductively slid in next to me. Vanessa had "come fuck me eyes." Eyes that grabbed ahold of me and had me wanting to smash my lips on hers. But technically, I was her boss, so I probably shouldn't let my dick lead in the situation.

"Hey, baby," I gave her a quick kiss on the cheek. "Did you miss me? How's business?"

"Don't I always," I loved the way she flirted with me. "It has been so busy around here lately. After the kickass summer we had last year, Damon decided he should a hire a few new girls. I was stoked when he asked me to sit in on the interview process. We interviewed about one hundred girls, watched forty dance, and brought ten back for a party night. We ended up choosing three new dancers," Vanessa's eyes got bright as

she explained all this to me. I knew when we hired Nessa she would be more than just a dancer if we could figure out how to use her assets. "O-M-G, Nathaniel, you would have died laughing if you could have seen some of these girls. There was one girl who had said that she has been here before on one of our theme nights and had a suggestion for us. You've heard of furries right? Well, she comes out with just the head of a fox costume on and this hideous orange thing on and does an entire pole dance to, of course, What Does the Fox Say? And the best part was her name, Fanny Fox."

"A furry? Can't say I've heard of that one. And by the sound of it, I'm sure I want to. So who are the new girls?" I asked looking around to see if I could spot any new faces.

"Why? You getting tired of me already?" she crawled into my lap and began kissing my neck. Vanessa was good at her job and knew how to keep her customers happy. But she also knew exactly where her lines were drawn, and I respected her for that. Other guys at The Cave have asked her out, but dating her clients was something she wouldn't do. That's the other reason I've never attempted to take it a step further with her.

"Of course not, baby. But like they say variety is the spice of life," I said, coming off completely cheesy.

"The only one working tonight is Jordyn. Young little college thing," Vanessa pointed to the stage. "Might be just your type, champ. Would you like to meet her?" she whispered in my ear.

"Sure. If you think she might be my type," I winked at

her as she went to pull Jordyn off the stage. I needed to remember to have a talk with Damon about Vanessa later. She might just be manager material.

Both Vanessa and Jordyn came back to my table with beers and Jack Daniels shots. "Ah, women after my own heart." Jordyn was undeniably gorgeous. She was tall, with sexy legs that I could imagine feeling incredible wrapped around my body. With the tight lace corset she wore you could see her perfect hourglass shape. And those baby blue eyes that had this crazy sparkle to them. Introductions and typical strip club small talk were made. Where are you from? Do you have a day job? All that bullshit.

'So Hott' by Kid Rock started playing over the speakers. Vanessa and Jordyn gave each other this sexy as fuck look and I knew I was in trouble. Jordyn crawled up and straddled both Vanessa and myself, one leg in between my legs and the other between Nessa's. Jordyn leaned into Vanessa and kissed her softly from her chest all the way up to her lips. Vanessa's tongue invaded Jordyn's mouth like she couldn't get enough of the way she tasted. A deep, throaty moan came from Vanessa and Jordyn's thigh squeezed tighter around my leg. Jordyn sat up and leaned over and gently nibbled on my earlobe. I felt my dick beginning to press against the side of my jeans. She slowly stood up and moved her tight body directly in front of me. She spun around, bent over to take a sip of her neon green drink. Jordyn's ass was two perfectly shaped globes, it was taking everything I had to not press my face into her and bite that cute little butt.

As she took a drink with one hand, she reached around

behind her and pulled on the string that was laced up the back of her black and red lace corset and her top fell. Usually, I preferred natural tits- big, small, perky, or saggy—it didn't matter to me. But between growing up in Los Angeles and now living in Las Vegas, real boobs were hard to come by. Jordyn began to sensually dance in between Vanessa and I, dragging her nails up and down both of our chests. Fuck it was hot. She continued to dance her way closer to me until she was completely straddling my lap. Vanessa stood up to leave. "Where are you going?" I asked, grabbing her wrist, still unable to keep my eyes off Jordyn.

"Enjoy," Vanessa smirked before walking out and leaving Jordyn and me there alone. This girl could rock her hips like no one I had ever felt before. She continued to grind into my lap and with each shift of her hips, thrusting her sex, there was no stopping, no self-control and my dick continued to grow. She knew what she was doing, it was as if she read my mind and knew just how I liked it and what turned me on. With each bite of her lip and every moan she let escape, I could barely restrain myself from touching her back or better yet pounding the fuck out of her pussy right then and there.

From our conversation earlier, I knew Jordyn was new to Vegas and currently single. "So," I leaned in close to whisper in her ear, "How are you getting home tonight, sexy?"

"I was hoping you had the answer to that, baby," she answered in a raspy voice that spoke of sex and trouble.

After that night, Jordyn and I were inseparable. If we weren't working, then we were fucking. Damon wasn't thrilled that I was seeing one the girls, but as long as it didn't interfere with business there wasn't much he could say about it. I loved watching my girl strip. Something about it gave me a rush straight to my dick. She wiggled that cute little ass and flaunted those beautiful tits for other guys, but it was my mouth all over her body each night.

It didn't take me long to fall head over heels for Jordyn. She got me. She understood my love for poker and my late nights, she understood my enjoyment of strippers, and she understood how to make my dick happy. Four months into our relationship, Jordyn got pregnant. It wasn't in our plan, but ultimately we were thrilled. At twenty-four, I wasn't sure if I was ready to start a family, but I really didn't have a choice anymore. Nine months later, Ella Marie Sims was born.

After the birth of Ella, Jordyn had made the decision not to dance anymore. She wanted to pursue a nursing career. I was all for my girl following any dream she had. Jordyn got accepted to the nursing program at San Diego State University. Being the loyal and supportive boyfriend I was, we picked up and moved to San Diego, California. Being away from the card tables meant more traveling for me to be able to make money playing poker. You can't make shit playing at the Indian casinos they had out there.

The traveling ultimately created a huge point of contention between Jordyn and myself. We were constantly fighting about how much time I was spending away from home. When I first met Jordyn, she seemed to understand what being in a relationship with a professional poker player meant. After Ella was born, she didn't seem to have that same understanding. I wanted her to be able to go to nursing school and not have to work so she could spend more time with our daughter. Therefore, I needed to play in the big money tournaments, which were not located in San Diego.

Our relationship continued that way for years. Even though we fought like the best of them, we remained together. Somewhere in my messed up head I believed it was better for Ella if her parents were together. So for her sake, we endured the distance that seemed to be dragging us apart. I loved Jordyn, I really did. Did I think she was my forever? No. That's probably why I never married her. But Jordyn and I had a daughter, and we were pretty damn good in bed together.

I'd been in Vegas playing a week long tournament for television right before Ella's fourth birthday. I lost it all on day three and asked if I could do all my post interviews early. I was able to make it home a day earlier than expected. I didn't call Jordyn to tell her, instead I wanted to give her and my J-Ella Bean an early birthday surprise.

Little did I know the surprise would be on me that night when I came home. Upon entering our apartment and I could hear Jordyn's soft moans coming from our bedroom. Hell yes, I loved to hear my girl getting herself off. It wasn't an unusual thing for her to do. Pleased that Ella was obviously in bed for the night, I decided to sneak in and kiss her goodnight before I kissed all over her mommy. As I looked down in her bed I realized Ella wasn't there. What the fuck? Where was my daughter? Jordyn probably took her to her parents' so she could have some time to get ready for the party. I hated having to be away so much.

I couldn't wait to see sink my cock deep into my girl. Even though we fought, she was still my girl and I loved her. As I was walking down the hall, I heard two sets of moans. I stopped to listen. That was not Jordyn. She had a movie on too. Even fucking better. I stripped down naked in the hallway, and started stroking my cock. I wanted to be hard as soon as I went into the room.

"Fuck yes, Alex! Harder! Harder!" Jordyn screamed. What the fuck? I opened the door of my bedroom, dick in hand, to see Jordyn on her hands and knees and Alex, wearing a goddamn strap-on, was fucking her from behind.

"Well, welcome fucking home to me," I yelled as I watched the two quickly jump up from my bed and grab their robes. You would think I would be excited to come home and find two women in my bed. But I knew Alex from The Cave in Vegas. She was not someone who I wanted in bed, in my home, or in my girl. "You two were fucking made for each other. Where's Ella?"

"At my mom's," Jordyn answered, never looking up from her feet. I backed up to leave. "Can we at least talk about this?"

"Nope. Nothing to say. I'm going to go pick up Ella for the night. We will be here tomorrow in plenty of time for the party. And that bitch better not be here," I demanded, pointing to Alex.

After that night, I swore on anything I had that I would never date a stripper again.

Hot for Teacher

After my first night at *The Cave*, all my emotions were tied up in a huge ball right in the pit of my stomach. I was scared to death to get on stage and dance. I'd always been shy but that night, with more of my body exposed than ever, I felt confident. I didn't dance, but in my barely there outfit, I allowed myself to be free. Now I just needed to figure out a way to let this new found confidence beat the nerves.

"So, what'd ya think?" Vanessa asked as we were walking out of the club. "Can you do this?"

"I think I can. It might take me a little bit of time to take it all in but I know I can do this," I quietly replied.

"You need to have a bit more confidence in yourself, girl. In this extremely low cut V-neck top thing you have on, there wasn't a man, or a woman for that matter, that could take their eyes of you and your girls and you weren't even dancing. You were damn sexy tonight," she said as she slid her finger down my chest.

"Really?" I'd never seen myself as sexy. I was the kindergarten teacher or the wife. I guess I never thought of myself as someone who could even be sexy. Lucas was always more concerned with the end product rather than making me feel desired.

"Damn straight! You ready for Stripper 101 tonight, Teach?" Vanessa shouted as she cranked up the stereo of her Wrangler and ripped out of the parking lot.

There were a few cars in Vanessa's driveway when we pulled up. I recognized Rose's truck and assumed the rest of the cars belonged to the other girls. "Stripper 101, huh? This could be interesting," I mumbled as we walk in.

"Holy shit," I mumbled when I stepped into her place. Chairs were set up in the living room for dances and there was some weird lap dance tutorial video playing on the big screen. In Vanessa's dressing room, all the outfits I purchased the day before were laying across the table, and there was an area set up in the corner for pictures. "Oh. Hell. No." When I looked across the hall into Vanessa's bedroom, I noticed a stripper pole in the middle of the room. Nice, girl!

"Hey biotch! You ready for some fun tonight?" Rose jumped in front of me out of nowhere and handed me my regular vodka and cranberry.

"More than you know," I answered grabbing my drink and walking out of the room with a smirk.

"What the hell is that supposed to mean?" Rose shouted.

I handed Jade my phone and told her to play *Closer* by Nine Inch Nails. "Rose, sit your ass down in that chair." My best friend was the only one I think I could do this with for the first time. I quickly sucked down the rest of my drink. "Alright, here goes nothing,"

The music started. I got down on my hands and knees and started crawling towards Rose. I threw my hair around in a sexy flip that guys seemed to go crazy for. I stopped just in front of her, sat on my knees and rubbed my hands up and down her legs as my body bounced up and down. I could see the surprised look on Rose's face as I started to dance in front of her. When I stood up, I ran my hands all the way up her body and straddled her lap. As I swayed my hips back and forth in front of Rose all the girls around me started to cheer me on. Lap dancing was all about moving your body in a way that mimics sex and actually fucking someone with your eyes.

"Is there something you need to tell me?" Rose asked, cocking her head to one side.

"I can dance," I laughed.

"Umm, obviously. Care to explain this sudden knowledge of lap dances?"

"Well," I started to climb off Rose's lap, "since my divorce, I needed to do something for me. Lucas had this weird aversion to strip clubs, and the last thing he ever did toward the end was make me feel sexy. And you know that I hate the gym, so I started going to Ms. Jewel's dance studio. You should see my ass work the pole."

"Looks like we can skip the dance lessons," Vanessa chuckled. "On to the ensembles!"

The girls reluctantly pushed me into the dressing room to start trying on outfits. "Fine," I huffed, "but what's the point of the pictures?"

"You want to make a lot of money fast right?" Ashlynn asked. I nodded. "Well, then you need to look like an eleven every fuckin' night."

"She's right," Rose chimed in. "Even I did the pictures. The girls will help you match up outfits that make your body look the best. And you're even more of a challenge because we need to match wig and contact colors to change your appearance. The pictures will allow you to see the outfits you like."

"Alright, ladies. I trust you. Let's do this!" Clothes, shoes, and wigs started flying everywhere.

"So why did Nathan hightail it out of the club when you introduced him to Vaughn?" Ashlynn asked Vanessa.

"He started following the Vaughn Haley Instagram after he drove us back to the hotel after the dirty-thirty!" Rose jumped in to answer.

"Wait! Nathan was there?" Ashlynn squealed. "And where did this Vaughn Haley come from?"

"Yeah, baby, he was. We may need to have a chat with him about that," Vanessa answered. "And I have no idea why he left so quickly."

"What's Mr. Nathaniel Sims's story?" I inquired.

Vanessa turned to me. "Nathan is a regular. He's a professional poker player and comes to *The Cave* to unwind. He's been coming there since it opened. He and Damon have been best friends since college. The rest is his to tell." Something told me there was more to the story by the look on Vanessa's face.

The rest of the night was a blur of outfit changes, camera flashes and pole dances. For a world that I felt so apart from two weeks ago, now it seemed normal. It was time to start living my life for me.

**

My first week at *The Cave* passed in a flash. My confidence was slowly building and I was really beginning to enjoy what I was doing. For the first couple of days, I just worked the floor and the poles around the club. Damon had been patient with me, letting me ease my way into it. I think Vanessa and Rose may have talked to him about my situation.

During that first week, I had the guy all the girls warned me about. He seemed harmless enough when I approached up to the booth. Older gentleman, I'd put him in his sixties, balding, gold chains, and to top it all off, a baby blue track suit. A track suit hides nothing. The old guy was the first customer I had that I could actually see his erection growing under his pants. I would love to say that was the worst of it, but it wasn't. I took my top off and danced topless across his lap. Three grunts later, I unfortunately felt the old guy all over my leg. It was horrible. It's all about "paying your dues" as the new girl, as Ashlynn put it to me.

Each night I kept my eye out for Nathaniel, but he hadn't come back to the club all week. I wasn't sure if I was disappointed or relieved about that. He seemed like a nice guy the night of my birthday. Well, what I can remember of it.

He started following "me" on social media that same night, yet has never messaged me. I think guys can be just as complicated as women sometimes. I resisted the urge to Google him, even though it was killing me not to. But something about the way Vanessa told me it was his story made me want to wait.

I had the next two days off, and being the obsessive kind of person I was, I began looking up every strip tease video I could find on the internet. Even though I'd been dancing for a while now, I had never actually taken off my clothes while doing it. So this was all new to me. I decided if I was going to make money I needed to get my ass up on stage and make "Vaughn Haley" come to life. Vanessa and I had been working on my first signature character stage dance. Knowing I was still battling a bit of nerves, we decided to do a duo dance.

We were scheduled to go on at ten-thirty on Friday, and were backstage getting ready. "Holy shit, the house is packed out there," Ashlynn said as she came running in the dressing room. "Somehow word got out that you were doing a special performance, Nessa."

"Hmmm. I wonder how that could have happened," Vanessa raised her eyebrows at Ashlynn.

"Dunno," she just shrugged her shoulders and smiled. "Damn baby, you look hot tonight." Ashlynn commented as she kissed Vanessa. It's wasn't something they usually flaunted at work, but there was no reason to hide in front of me. Vanessa had on a skimpy as hell leather bondage dress. It was almost completely open down the front, covering just enough boob to make it sexy not slutty, connected down the middle by only a couple of spaghetti straps. With the six-inch thigh high vinyl hooker boots, the outfit definitely was complete.

We heard the D.J. call us to the stage and I knew this was it. I could feel the nerves sweeping over my body and all I wanted to do was puke. Despite what you might think, even experienced girls still felt this way before heading on stage. You'd think that information would have calmed my nerves, but it didn't. It was like my first time having sex all over again but worse. Much worse. All I kept thinking was don't fall. Don't make a fool out of yourself because living with mom and Stuart would be much worse.

The music cued, the stage was completely dark, which was Vanessa's idea. She thought it would calm the storm of the shock of what I was about to do. Not sure if I'd thanked her for the brilliant idea, but I would because it worked. When the crowd started to hear the guitar and drum beats of Van Halen they went crazy knowing what was about to come next. I knew every man out there had that one hot teacher they fantasized about—and that night I got to be part of their fantasy. I was in awe as I watched Vanessa walk onstage with such grace and ease, yet so sexy and confident.

The spotlights came down and focused on Vanessa in her crazy leather outfit. She was sitting on a teacher's desk with a long whip in her hand. Vanessa makes me hot and I wasn't even into girls. But she also gave me a smile letting me know I've got this. She had a way of making you feel comfortable being up there next to her.

The lights came to me next. I was wearing the classic short little school girl outfit. We went with the long brown wig to perfectly match my eyes, done up in those yankable pigtails. I didn't want to wear contacts my first night on stage because I wanted to see everything clearly. My glasses clearly fit the theme better. It was a fast paced song so Vanessa told me to have fun with it, reminding me that our theme was "hot for teacher with a rowdy student." Our plan was for me to be the little brat and she to be the teacher who makes sure I got what was coming to me.

As I started to dance, I glanced up in the VIP booths and there he was. Nathaniel was in his booth, leaning over the railing watching us. He hadn't been there all week and picked tonight to show his ass back up. What the hell was his thing with keeping his distance? And why did it seem like he was watching me? Maybe he really was one of those creepy, stalker guys. He wanted a show? I was going to give him a fucking show.

"Let's do this," I mouthed as I moved around the desk. I threw all the papers to the ground, and started to crawl across the top of it on my hands and knees. Slowly I stood up and started undoing the buttons of my white tied up shirt. I revealed the green plaid bra that matched the micro skirt I had on. The fish net thigh highs with the garter straps made me feel sexy as hell. All my nerves were gone. I felt like a pro, like a real dancer. Vanessa began to play her role as teacher and ordered me down, and of course that meant one of my magnificent squats right in front of her. I decided to play it up a bit and snagged my fingers down her straps. She grabbed me by my hair and pulled me off the desk and ordered me to bend over. I knew if I wanted to make money out here tonight I was going to have to let it all go. I made direct eye contact with Nathaniel. The heat coming from his stare made my insides coil.

"You wanted to watch, buddy," I whispered to myself. I gave him my back, reached around and unclasped the bra I was wearing. I pulled it off and threw it to the side. Feeling totally vulnerable, I looked to his booth, to find he was gone, nowhere to be seen. *What the fuck*? This fueled me even more. I continued to dance around stage flaunting myself more now than I thought I would have before. I made my way back over to the desk and bent over, leaving my tits completely exposed. Vanessa took the whip and gave me the spanking that I deserved. I liked—no I loved it. The crowd went nuts. It really amazed me at how much money was being thrown on stage and how much fun I had. A girl could get used to this!

After the song ended, we grabbed what we needed and ran off stage. "Oh. My. God. That was amazing!" I yelled as I hit the dressing room. "Did you see the attention we were getting?"

"*You* were getting, my dear," Vanessa corrected. "I was merely a background prop."

"Background prop my ass," I laughed. "So, did you happen to notice Nathaniel up in his booth? But he disappeared as I was taking my top off. He was up there watching and then just poof. Gone. It really fueled my fire tonight."

"Is that what happened out there? Well, whatever it is, keep it up. You made over a grand out there tonight," Vanessa informed me.

"*We* made a thousand," I reminded her.

"This was your character dance, you naughty little student. It's all yours, Vaughn." She handed me the money. "But don't let this thing with Nathaniel get under your skin. He's a regular, and friends with Damon, so figure it out. Put back on your naughty little schoolgirl uniform and get your ass up to his booth and go talk to him."

I went to Rose, grabbed a Flaming Doctor Pepper and took it up to his booth. I sat down next to him, lit the shot on fire and dropped it into the Stella. I watched him carefully as he drank the shot back. You couldn't help but notice the well-defined muscles in his tattoo covered arms. Damn the man was hot! Too bad I had to meet him as Vaughn and not Ryann. "Hi, Mr. Sims. I'm Vaughn, I believe we've met. A few times actually," I laughed. "Thanks for making sure I got back to the hotel the other night. I enjoyed my birthday a little too much." Damn, I was rambling.

"My pleasure. Gotta make sure Damon's girls get home safe right?" he said with a smug attitude.

"Well, I actually wasn't one of Damon's girls then. I'm new to dancing. Actually, I've only been dancing a week," I informed him.

"Hmmm…I didn't realize Damon was now hiring women in their thirties. Must be a new MILF thing," Nathaniel said looking me up and down. That one hit hard.

He was an asshole. Definitely not the sweet man that carried me to bed the other night. I could feel the tears starting to well up in my eyes. I needed to get the fuck away from him before he saw me cry. I'd be damned if I let another man take my power from me. "Goodnight, Mr. Sims. Enjoy your night here at *The Cave*," I snapped right before I got up to walk away. I knew there was an obvious hitch in my tone.

Nathaniel put his hand on my leg as I started to stand. "I'm sorry," he said. "You're just not who I thought you were. And, please, my friends here at the club call me Nathan."

What was that supposed to mean? Pulling myself together, I stood up and peered down at him. "Well, *Mr. Sims*," I replied scathingly, "we're not friends. And all I can say is that the same goes for you. You are definitely *not* who I thought you were." I walked downstairs, and grabbed a shot from Rose at the bar. I needed to dance. I would not let this jerk get the best of me.

Jade came and grabbed me, telling me there was group of football players at one of the VIP booths that were smoking hot. They were a bunch of NFL guys from back east and one of the players who was apparently into strippers and porn stars had requested the presence of the naughty new student at their table tonight.

"Oh this should be fun," I said to Rose before being dragged away by Jade. I had always been more of a baseball girl myself but it was time to discover some new passions. I looked up and saw that the football players were in the booth that was adjacent to the asshole's. This might be more fun than I thought. A pro NFL player had to be better than some sleazy old guy in a tracksuit, right?

The men introduced themselves, and of course I didn't recognize any of them. Unless you do an insurance commercial I probably didn't know who you were. But I could tell that these guys were money. That was my whole purpose, to come here and make money, not to get all flustered by a hot tattooed poker player. Jade, Ashlynn, and I hung out with them for the rest of the evening. Surprisingly, for the most part, all they wanted to do was have a decent conversation. But after more and more alcohol kept flowing, the more the guys kept talking about what they came to see.

Jade and Ash began kissing and touching each other and most of the guys seemed to be pretty into that. For me, I was just not quite sure how far I could actually go with another girl. Don't get me wrong, women are beautiful and tits actually turn me on, but I have yet to actually make-out with another woman. The ringleader, "G" as most of the other guys called him, seemed to be more focused in on me. He pulled me down on his lap and whispered in my ear, "Is there somewhere more private we can go?" I instantly felt myself get wet between the legs. I knew he was paying me, but damn this man made me feel sexy.

We stood and I grabbed his hand. The only way into the private rooms was to walk right in front of Mr. Sims' booth. Well, there was another way but that would mean walking downstairs and across the dance floor. I smiled at G and we sauntered right past Nathaniel and into the rooms. I could almost feel the anger coming off his glare. Again, something about that man almost fueled the naughty streak in me.

G and I found one of the private booths, and again it seemed like mostly just conversation. I'd take talking with him any day. But damn this guy was fine; I couldn't help but admire his tall, muscular frame, dark eyes, and long hair. Vanessa told me some guys are like this. Almost out of nowhere, G scooped me up in his lap and unhooked my bra top in one quick move. *Smooth.* I slowly shimmed the bra off of my arms exposing my girls completely to him.

"Are these what you've been waiting to see?" I asked in what I think is a seductive, sexy voice.

"Damn, Vaughn from a distance your tits look good, but up close they are beautiful," G said to me in his Boston accent as he ran his finger down my chest attempting to touch my breast.

Even though I knew he was a VIP, I politely pushed his hands back down away from me. "Ah ah ah," I swiped my finger at him. "We don't do the hands on thing here, G."

"This is VIP, I was told that anything goes up here in these rooms," the football player argued back with me.

"Maybe with some girls, but not with me, hot stuff. I can go get you someone else if you like or I can I can give you one hell of a dance with these beautiful tits," I sassed while rubbing my already fully erect nipples.

"Mmmm, baby. Let's see what you've got," G whispered back to me.

Thirty minutes later, I escorted G back to his table and thanked him for a wonderful time. It was almost closing time and I was ready to start finishing my stuff up for the night. I look around for Nathaniel and of course, he was nowhere to be found. Typical, disappeared again.

Scars

I'd avoided the club for the past week because I knew I couldn't handle seeing Vaughn dancing there. I'd just been wasting my time in different poker games around Vegas. When I met her the night of her birthday, I didn't peg Vaughn as a dancer. There was just something different about her. I knew I couldn't avoid the situation forever but I wasn't ready to deal with the fact that the woman I'd been dreaming about for the past week was a fucking stripper. That must have been where I'd seen her before when I got the feeling I knew her from somewhere.

I made my way up to my reserved booth and kept my eyes open for Vaughn. I wasn't sure what I was going to say to her but I needed to say something. After a half an hour, and already too many drinks, I still had yet to see her anywhere. The stage lights went dark and the D.J. called Vaughn and Vanessa to the stage. No. Fucking. Way. Just thinking about those two insanely hot women, that I've had multiple dreams about, dancing together was making me hard. *Hot for Teacher* by Van Halen blasted through the club. That little school girl outfit Vaughn had on was incredible. I would love to shove my hands straight up that skirt and grab her ass as she wrapped those pretty little legs around me. We kept making eye contact and my dick had totally forgotten she was a stripper and we don't fuck around with strippers anymore.

"Wait a second…Van Halen. Vaughn Haley, Really now?" That shit almost made me laugh until I realized I was pretty damn positive someone had lied to me. It was at that moment, Vaughn reached around to unsnap her bra. There was no way the first time I'd see her tits was the same as three hundred other guys. I was too pissed to enjoy them anyways at that moment. Better time than any to go take a piss. When I heard the song had finally ended I made my way up to my booth to hopefully spend some time with Ashlynn. If nothing else, at least I could get a massage. But it seemed like all the regulars were booked with some big shot VIP party. Shit. But I guess that's how we made money.

As I sat back down, I saw Vaughn making her way toward me, drink in hand. The last thing I needed was another drink. She tried to talk to me but only asshole spewed from my lips. I felt lied to, and humiliated by her and Rose. Rose knew how I felt about dating strippers. The more she tried to be nice the bigger of a jerk I became. I knew I crossed the line when I said something about her being a MILF. I hated to see Vaughn fight back the tears. But I wanted her to hurt the way I was hurting.

Not long after, I saw Jade go to the main bar, talk to Vaughn and drag her up to the VIP party she was catering to tonight. Did they really have to be right next me? I guess I could have just gotten up and left, but there was no way in hell my jealousy would have let me do that. I could tell Vaughn was being extra flirty with the guy. I could actually hear her. Was she doing this just to get to me? When she stood up with Mr. NFL, I recognized him immediately. Though he was great on the field, off the field he had a dirty reputation with the ladies. I couldn't believe Vaughn would actually go into the private rooms with anyone so soon. That was it for me. I needed some air.

I walked out to my bike and grabbed a joint I kept hidden in the side compartments. Some may not agree with this method to control my anger, but it was better than hitting a wall. I took a few hits and it was all I needed to feel my body relax. When finished, I returned to Damon's office and started scanning the security monitors.

"Something you're looking for I should know about?" Damon asked, curious.

"Has Vaughn come out of the private room? She's in there with G and I know he has quite a reputation with the ladies and she's new to this," I asked trying to act more concerned than pissed off.

"I have no idea. But there's security in there if anything goes wrong and Vaughn knows how to handle herself," Damon answered. His brow furrowed and his eyes squinted, showing me he was both irritated and perplexed by my attitude. "What the hell is going on with you and Vaughn?"

"Nothing. I was a dick to her and I need to apologize. She went off with G and I got concerned. These are my girls too, Damon," I reminded him.

Damon knew there was more to it than that. He'd known me too long not to. "I lost two good girls because of you once, don't go fucking around on me again. Even if she is only here for the summer."

"That was a long damn time ago, will you stop bringing that shit up? And both of those girls weren't any good and you know that. Plus, you know how I feel about strippers," I continued to argue with him. What did he mean she would only be here for the summer? My mind was fucking racing now. Even though my head kept telling me to stay away, that she's no different than any other stripper, every other part of my body was completely drawn to her.

I waited in the back office until I saw Vaughn starting to make her way to the parking lot with Bobby, our security guard. Now that I'd sobered up, I needed to apologize for what I said to her earlier. That wasn't me. That was anger and disappointment, mixed with way too many shots.

I stepped out of Damon's office as they passed by. "Vaughn, can we talk please?" I asked her.

"Nope, I really don't have anything to say to you. Bobby, can you please take me to my car?" She continued to walk right past me.

"I've got it from here, Bobby," my tone left no room for argument. Bobby was Damon's younger brother, and one of the few people who knew I was a silent partner. That knowledge was what most certainly had him obeying and going inside to wait for the other girls.

"You're joking, right? What, because you're some famous poker player and the boss's friend, people around here jump at your command?" Vaughn was beginning to yell at me and I could tell she was upset. *Great, I've done it again.*

"Calm down, butterfly. Just let me walk you to your car." I placed my hand on the small of her back and gently guided her out the door. "Which car is yours?" She pointed to the sleek looking purple Dodge Challenger. Okay, I wasn't expecting that one. She noticed the surprised look on my face.

"My ex liked muscle cars. I couldn't help but fall in love with them also," Vaughn explained. Ex? That was damn good news to hear, but the way she talked about him made it sound like she was still hung up on him. *Damn it.* Why did I even care?

"Look, butterfly. I'm sorry for my behavior tonight. That wasn't me. The comment I said to you was horrible and if I could take it back I would," I apologized as we stopped next to her car.

"You can't and it's fine," she lied, her right hand digging around in her purse; doing her best to avoid eye contact with me.

Oh, that is not good. A woman saying things are fine is the kiss of death. "Please look at me." I gently lifted her chin up to meet my eyes. "I really didn't mean it. Let me take you to go get some breakfast so I can explain." Doubt clouded her eyes, but I could tell she was the type of girl that needed an explanation.

"The girls told me I shouldn't go out with clients," she answered, a cute smile tugging at her lips.

"Good thing I'm more than just a client. Give me your

keys. I only have my bike tonight and we'll need to get a helmet for you before I can give you a ride."

The laugh that came from her almost caught me off guard. "Yeah, I don't think so, nuts. No one drives my car but me." Nuts? Damon. I needed to remember to kick his ass.

"Really now? A woman in control. I like that," I said as I climbed in the passenger seat. "I know a diner at the end of the strip that serves some amazing pancakes. Sound good?"

"Nope. I have a better idea," she said as she drove down the strip. She flipped on the radio and *Why Can't I* by Liz Phair came blaring through the speakers. Slightly awkward, but weirdly appropriate. She hopped on the freeway and I had not a clue where my butterfly was taking me, but I was definitely intrigued. Part of me wanted to ask where we were going but I was enjoying the mystery of her.

During the twenty-minute drive there wasn't much conversation. Vaughn was definitely a music person. About every other minute she was changing the radio stations. She had the windows down, which had her hair blowing in her face, but she continued singing along to every song. My butterfly was a fun person to watch. I still had no idea where she was taking me when we pulled into a condo complex. However, when we pulled into her garage, the lightbulb went on. Holy shit, this girl took me to her house. *Fuck!* Damn, maybe this girl is more than a stripper. *Shit, when did my instincts get so bad?*

"My dog hasn't been let out all night, and why pay for pancakes when I can make some excellent ones right here?

Just don't get any crazy ideas, nuts." With that she got out and ran inside the house. *Well, didn't I feel like a dumbass.*

I sat there for a second trying to regain my thoughts when I heard her dog starting to bark. From the sounds of it, it was a large dog. She popped her out of the garage door, "You're not afraid of dogs are you?" Shit, I guess I'd been sitting there longer than I realized.

I jumped out of her car and made my way into her place. Cute little place, not really what you'd expect a stripper's home to look like. But then again, I'd never been to a dancer's place besides Jordyn's, so how the hell would I know? Vaughn's place was decorated in a beach style, surfboards, seashells, and lots of turtles. It reminded me a lot of where I grew up back in California. I had to laugh when I saw the big pit bull with its nose pressed up against the glass of the patio door.

"That's Roxy. She's my four-year-old rescue. If dogs don't bother you, I'd love to let her in. But I warn you, guard your toes," she laughed as she let the rambunctious dog inside. Immediately, the crazy dog ran over to me and started licking the toes of my boots. "I have no idea. She's weird." Vaughn shrugged and walked back into the kitchen and started pulling everything out to make me breakfast.

"Hold it right there, butterfly. I asked you to breakfast. Let me cook. Plus, you worked all night," I said as I guided her around the counter and into one of the bar stools. She threw her hands up in defeat. I could see the surprise in her face, which had me wondering if her ex never did anything like that for her before.

I loved having her brown eyes watch me as I cooked. I wasn't a great chef, but I knew my way around a kitchen. Being single for so long kind of forced me into it. You can only eat at the casinos so many nights a week.

"Why do you keep calling me butterfly? Is it because of my tattoos?" Vaughn asked.

"No, but someday I would like to learn what those mean. Okay, I'm about to get all Bill Nye the Science Guy here on you now." That made her chuckle. "When you think about a butterfly, it's constantly changing. Every time you see it, it looks different. It goes from a caterpillar, to a cocoon, to the butterfly. Not one time, ever less beautiful than before, just always different. Each time I see you, you seem to be a different person. So you are my butterfly."

A tear slid down her cheek. Damn, the last thing I wanted to do was make her cry, but I'd definitely impressed myself with my explanation, "Don't cry, beautiful," I whispered as I wiped the tear from her cheek.

"That was one of the most beautiful things anyone has ever said to me."

"Oh, only one of the most beautiful things huh? Looks like I may have my work cut out for me," I teased, wanting to see her smile again.

"Will you excuse me for just a second please?" Vaughn hopped down and went back to her bedroom. I really hoped I didn't upset her more. It was not my intention for this morning's breakfast. I continued cooking hoping she liked everything I was making. She wasn't there to ask and I really didn't want to make her upset anymore than I already had. *Blueberry pancakes, eggs, and bacon it is.*

My butterfly came walking back into the kitchen in a pair of short jean shorts, a Miranda Lambert concert tank top, and her long blonde hair pulled back in a ponytail. The thick makeup the girls at the club wore, was gone. "Hi. I'm Ryann. I have a summer job at *The Cave*," she held out her hand. And there's my blonde beauty.

"Hi, Ryann. My name's Nathaniel, but my friends call me Nathan. I play cards for a living. I really hope we can be friends."

"I would like that," she whispered, her eyes on mine.

We spent the next couple hours getting to know each other with small talk. Dancer or not, my gut was telling me there was something more to her. Wisely, I knew not to push for more information than she'd given so far. But hopefully, Ryann and I would have those talks later. We actually had a lot in common. We'd both kill for sushi anytime of the day, we were dog people, and were both from California. She was from northern, and I was from southern. I made her promise to never use the word "hella" in front of me. I think I might have created a monster.

As the sun was starting to come up, exhaustion began to play across Ryann's face. She started to yawn and her eyes were fluttering closed. "Hey, butterfly, let's get you to bed." I picked her up like I did the night of her birthday and carried her back to her bedroom. Tucking her head in the crook of my neck, I got a whiff of her coconut scented hair. The scent was becoming my newest addiction. I gently set her down on the bed, and tucked the covers over her. Hesitating for a few more moments, I watched to make sure she was comfortable, then turned to leave.

"Where are you going?" Ryann mumbled. "We left your bike at the club." She rolled over to look at me. "Come lay down with me."

Damn, this woman was killing me. "As tempting as that offer is, I think I might take the couch for a couple hours. I don't trust myself in bed with you, butterfly." I kissed her again on her forehead and left her room.

In the living room, Roxy was spread across the couch, snoring. Ryann told me this was Roxy's house and she gets the privilege of living here. We'd been fighting with that crazy dog for the couch all morning. I decided to make myself comfortable on the recliner chair and tried to catch a few hours of sleep before I called Vanessa to come get me. If anyone could help me figure this shit out it's my Nessa. Her and I have had our ups and down but she's always been in my corner.

Once I closed my eyes, all I heard was Roxy snoring on the couch across from me. I had a beautiful woman who invited me to share her bed with her in the next room, and instead I was sharing the living room with her dog. I grabbed my phone.

Me: Nes—I'm at Vaughn's. Come get me please. My

bike's at the club.

Vanessa: WTH? Ok. When?

Me: Now...this dog snores like crazy.

Forty-five minutes later I got the text that Vanessa was here. I left the note I wrote Ryann on the kitchen counter, and quietly snuck out, making sure I locked the door behind me. The second I climbed in Vanessa's car she started screaming at me.

"I know you and Vaughn had some kind of argument last night and you said some awful things to her. But do you really think going home with her, calling her a dog, and then calling me for your walk of shame was the best to do, you idiot!"

By the time she was finished, I was trying not to laugh. "Are you finished?" I asked. Vanessa nodded, but her eyes still flashed daggers at me. "I was talking about her actual dog, Roxy. She offered to let me get some sleep in her bed, and in my gentlemanly ways, I declined and offered to sleep on the couch."

"Oh. Sorry." I explained to her that I apologized and offered to take her to get something to eat but instead we came back to her place, ate, talked and got to know each other a little.

When we pulled up in front of the club, she shut her car off and stared at me. "Do you like Vaughn, Nathan?" Hmm. Vanessa was still calling Ryann Vaughn. I wondered how much Vanessa really knew about her.

"I don't know. I know I'd like to get to know her better. What's her story, Nessa?" I asked.

"Just like I told her about you. It's her story to tell. I will tell you this. She's not like the other girls. Give her time. Now scoot. Just like Vaughn, I have the next two days off and need some rest." Vanessa winked at me and pushed me out of the car.

"Thanks, babe. I really do owe you one."

On my ride home that morning, I kept thinking about Vanessa's hint that Ryann had the next two days off. *I think I may just need to take advantage of that situation.*

After a few hours of sleep, I woke up with my mind still racing. I had a nice time with Ryann the night before. It just sucked that I literally had no idea how to move forward. When it came down to it, she was a stripper. Since Jordyn, I've been adamant about not dating strippers. But I should know by now I can't judge every dancer by my ex-slut's standards. Both Damon and Ryann mentioned that this was her summer job. So what was her regular job? Was she leaving Las Vegas after the summer, or just *The Cave*?

I wasn't going to find out anything unless I made that move. I didn't have to date her or have sex with her. Vanessa and I were friends, so why couldn't I be friends with Ryann? Right? Who was I trying to kid? I wanted to be much more than her friend.

Me: Good afternoon butterfly. Hope you got a good morning's sleep.

Ryann: Nathan?

Me: Is there someone else who calls you butterfly?

Ryann: Nope just you nuts. I did sleep well. I was bummed to come out and find you already gone.

Me: Couldn't sleep. Roxy snores. Lol. Do you have any plans tomorrow?

Ryann: Only my usual day off errands. Are you sure you want to be seen around Vegas with a MILF?

Me: Oh that one hurt. Of course I do. Remember what MILF stands for! ☻

The texting went quiet for a few minutes. In my effort to make up for being a jackass the other night, I most likely just upset her again. I really did need to work on not doing that.

Ryann: Maybe this is a bit presumptuous, but would you like to come over for dinner tonight? I am tired of eating alone and I figured we could finish our conversation from this morning.

Me: I feel the same way. What time would you like me to come over?

Ryann: Maybe around 7. Bring your swim trunks!

Me: Sounds good. See you tonight.

Well, I definitely wasn't expecting that. I knew I wanted to get to know her better, but I had definite hesitations. I had to remind myself that Ryann was not Jordyn. Choosing not to explore the apparent connection we had between us due to being burned by some other girl in the same profession would just be stupid on my part. That would be like someone not liking me because some other person beat them in cards. Ryann was beautiful, and there was something special about her. I owed it to both of us to see where things might go.

Not wanting to seem too eager, I waited until quarter after seven to arrive at Ryann's house. When I pulled up in front of her condo, I actually got a nervous feeling in my stomach, like I was in fucking high school or something. I grabbed the bouquet of sunflowers and the bottle of wine, and made my way to her door. As soon as I knocked, Roxy began barking like crazy. Ryann answered the door in a barbeque apron that said "Kiss the Cook". She had no idea how damn bad I wanted to do that. But right now, we were starting with this "friend" thing.

"Hey, nuts!" she greeted me with a happy smile, wrapping me in a surprisingly big hug.

"Hi, butterfly. I'm gonna have to kill Damon!" I said as I walked in.

"Why?"

"For telling you about my college nickname," I answered.

"Damon didn't tell me anything," she replied while walking to the back yard to tend to the barbeque. "Your Instagram name is @IGottheNuts21. And then you just followed me but never messaged me or liked anything so I just figured you were nuts," she joked.

I came up from behind her while she was turning the steaks, and put my arms around her waist. "You better be careful, I might just be nuts." I gave her a soft kiss on the back of her neck. The moan she let out was so sweet, it left me with the desire to kiss that spot over and over again.

"How do you like your steak?" she asked.

"Medium please. First pancakes and now steak, my two favorite things. A woman after my damn stomach," I laughed.

"Well, technically you made me pancakes so we're going to have to see how you like mine," she replied with a sly grin.

Nice and Slow

Even though Nathan had a tendency to be an asshole, there was something about him that kept drawing me in. I wanted to be the bitch who gave him the cold shoulder, and ignored how that sexy man made me wet between my thighs. But I couldn't. At the club, he'd said some things to me that pretty much brought me to tears, and I used G to piss him off. Or maybe make him jealous, I don't know. I just know I wanted him to hurt as much as I was. It seemed to work. When he came out of Damon's office and asked to walk me to my car I used my best "teacher face" to try and act mad. But honestly, with him it didn't work. When Nathan looked at me with those deep, golden hazel eyes my knees went weak and I giggled like a little school girl.

I knew when I invited him over I was asking for trouble. The man made me feel things I haven't felt in a long time. I was nervous and tongue tied and seemed to have a permanent smile around him. Nathan had this knack for getting under my skin. He could go from being the sweetest guy ever to the asshole who avoided me at every turn. I wasn't sure what his problem was but by inviting him over I hoped to figure him out a little bit.

I knew I was lonely. I missed having a man in my life,

and it wasn't just the physical connection either. I missed sharing meals with someone; missed arguing with someone over what to watch on television; I even missed the toilet seat being left up.

Nathan was the first guy that had even looked my way since my divorce, and there was a good possibility I was just seeing what I hoped to see. There was just one major problem. He wasn't looking at me. He was looking at my stripper persona, Vaughn. *Holy fuck, I can't believe I have a stripper name.* And he keeps calling me butterfly. I was sure it was a reference to my tattoos. If only he knew butterflies were a symbol for miscarriage, and my tattoos were a beautiful reminder that I had two angels waiting for me in heaven. At the same time, they were a symbol of something I could never have.

When he offered to make me breakfast, I was slightly in shock. I couldn't remember a time anyone had ever cooked for me before. Granted, I was with Lucas for the last nine years and he couldn't cook for shit, but still it was a sweet gesture. The guys I'd dated before weren't much better. Usually barbeque. That's how I learned. I could grill a mean steak, if I did say so myself. I just sat and stared in awe as he maneuvered his way around my kitchen.

I figured now was as good a time as any to ask him why he called me butterfly. I automatically assumed it was because of my tattoo, it was sort of obvious. Yet his answer shocked the hell out of me, but he was so right. I was a different person each time he saw me. The first time we met was my birthday and I was myself. Well, kind of. I looked like myself but Rose had introduced me as Vaughn. The next time was my first night at the club with the red wig, and then the night of my first stage performance as the naughty student.

I excused myself while he was beginning to cook and went into my bedroom. If I wanted Nathan to like me, he had to know me. The real me, Ryann Michelle McKennan—I needed to change that. But how much would I let him know? I couldn't tell him what I did for a living. No matter how much I liked him, it wasn't a chance I was willing to take. Did I lie or just omit any unnecessary information? *Slow down, Ryann.* Start with you physically. Blonde hair, brown eyes, jean shorts, and my Miranda tank. I'd just be myself...whoever that was.

For the next couple hours, we talked about all the random first date crap. As hard as I tried to focus on what he was saying, all I seemed to be able to see was the fine specimen of a man sitting next to me. He was in physically impeccable shape. His swollen biceps were well defined and etched with some amazing artwork. The tight fitting white t-shirt clearly showed the six-pack that he was trying to hide under there. The loose shorts that he was wearing showed his strong legs which were also covered in tattoos. My number one turn on when it came to guys was tattoos. Well done, sexy body art could be an instant panty dropper for me.

I was actually relieved when Nathan chose to sleep on the couch. Not that I hadn't wanted his fine body lying next to me as I slept, but it'd been so long since I'd had sex with anyone, beside B.O.B, that I didn't really trust myself with him. When I awoke, I was disappointed to find Nathan had left already, leaving me to wonder how he got home or back to his bike. When I went to make my morning coffee, I found a note from him, on the counter.

Butterfly~

I hope you slept well. I enjoyed getting to know you this morning. I want to know more. I will see you soon.

Nuts

The more time I spent with him, the more I likedwho he was. I didn't know much about him, but was eager to learn more. As much as I was interested, I still had reservations. For instance, why his personality kept going hot and cold on me? Honestly, it made me nervous. The sweet Nathan made me feel so safe already. Something about our situation made me want to jump all in. Well, as much as I could. Damn, I hated starting out a relationship, if that's what this was, with a lie. Fuck, I had no idea what to do. When in doubt, call Rose.

"Look, honey," she said, "I'm not sure what to tell you, but you have to do what feels right. Obviously, you two have a thing for each other. But his hot and cold attitude sucks. I know there's a story behind him. Get to know him. Hell, make it a summer fling. When you go back to your real life you can walk away knowing you had a kick ass summer."

As usual, Rose was right. It was time for me to stop feeling sorry for myself and enjoy life a little. Having that teacher instinct in me, I'd always had the need to plan out everything before I did it. Always making sure that one foot was carefully placed in front of the other. It was time to throw caution to the wind. Well at least for the next couple months. I grabbed my phone and logged into Instagram. I found @IGotTheNuts21 and followed him back. Step one.

Later that afternoon, as I was doing my usual day off cleaning, I heard my text message alert. Butterfly? This must be Nathan but how did he get my number? He must have gotten it from one of the girls at the club. I wished they wouldn't give out my number without asking me. That was kind of sketchy. Then I remembered I left my phone on the counter this morning. He must have texted himself before he left. He asked me out for tomorrow, but I knew I didn't want to wait that long to see him again. The summer would be over soon and then it was back to the reality of being a kindergarten teacher.

Rib-eye steaks, potatoes and corn on the barbeque were my specialty. I ran to the store and got everything I needed, including the ingredients to make the Flaming Doctor Pepper Nathan seemed to like so much. One my way home, I stopped by Rose's and asked her to teach me how to make the shot the same way she did. It was not nearly as hard to make as I thought it would, and I was shocked as hell to find out it doesn't even have any Dr. Pepper in it.

When I got home, I finished cleaning up my condo. Surprisingly, one dog could make a huge mess each week. I lit the few coconut and pineapple candles I had around my small living room. Something about the beachy scents brings me back to growing up in Santa Cruz. One of my favorite memories as a child was walking along the different beaches with my dad and collecting the unique looking shells and rocks that we would find together. On one trip to Maui, we found fresh coconuts and he showed me how to get the milk from them. We sat together on the beach and watched the surfers and drank our breakfast. He used to tell me he couldn't wait to teach his grandkids how to surf. That was our last vacation together. He passed away a few years ago. Every time I hear, *Somewhere Over the Rainbow* by IZ I believed my dad was having a surfing playdate with my angel babies.

Shortly after seven, I heard Nathan's Harley pull up in my driveway and right away Roxy started barking like crazy. Most of the time, the neighbors didn't complain because she only barked until she saw who was at the door. I had already started the barbeque and music playing through the patio speakers. Hopefully Nathan liked a little country. When I answered the door in my Kiss the Cook apron, I hoped he took that as a hint.

It was actually a really mild night for mid-June in Las Vegas, so we decided to take advantage of it and eat outside on the patio. The way the sunset made his golden eyes sparkle was memorizing. I found myself getting lost in what he was saying. Crap, I needed to stop and actually pay attention. Our conversation started out a bit awkward. There was no denying the shock my entire body felt every time he looked me, or how my knees went weak just by the slightest touch of his hand. We spent thirty minutes talking about what shows we have and haven't seen here in Vegas. Half of that was spent arguing about which Cirque du Soleil show was better.

"What brought you to *The Cave*?" Nathan asked.

That one caught me off guard. I slowly chewed the piece of steak in my mouth to give myself a minute to think. "My show is on hiatus for the summer. So I needed to pick up some extra cash. Bills don't pay themselves." Okay, I think I pulled that one off. Yet it almost looked like my answer disappointed him. I wondered why. Was being in a show such a bad thing?

"So why the different looks?" he continued.

I really should have given more thought to my cover story. "I enjoy being an actress. Each night I'm a different character out there on stage. The different looks help me play those parts. Plus, my show frowns upon side jobs." I remembered what Vanessa had told me about playing different parts.

"Are you enjoying working there?" He cocked an eyebrow.

At least that one I could answer honestly. "Yes and no. Do I like taking my clothes off for strangers? Not necessarily. But the money is great and it's getting me out of a difficult situation. I love the people I work with. I feel very safe at the club. And it's giving me more self-confidence than I've felt in years."

As we took our plates into the kitchen, I asked Nathan if he wanted to relax in the hot tub for a bit before they closed the pool area down for the night. By the smile he gave me, I think he liked my suggestion. "Go change. I'll be back in a couple of minutes." I ran back to my bedroom and started digging through my drawer of swim suits. Living in the land of pools for the last twelve years has taught me you needed a suit for every occasion. Tonight was sexy, but definitely not slutty. I decided on my simple black two piece. The bottoms fit my ass like a glove and are held together on the sides by two elastic straps. The tight triangle top held my 36Ds in just right. I threw on my pool cover-up, sandals, grabbed Nathan and I some towels and headed out to the living room to meet him.

He was in the kitchen, shirtless, pouring the wine he brought into my tall plastic Starbucks cups when I retuned. "I figured your pool doesn't allow glass, so I decided to use these instead."

"Perfect. Very impressive artwork there, nuts. You can really tell you're into your poker playing," I told him as I slowly ran my fingers up and down his back.

"I like all my tattoos to mean something. I don't understand the point of just random artwork," he explained to me as he finished pouring our drinks. My fingers stop on the name Ella Marie.

"Who's Ella Marie?" I asked, sensing his hesitation.

"Another night, butterfly," he whispered. I knew exactly what he meant by not answering and calling me butterfly at the same time. I wasn't ready to tell him about my tattoos either.

The walk to the pool was quiet. My community seemed especially tranquil that evening. During the summer my complex actually calmed down a bit because most of the college kids went home. I'd hoped we'd get lucky tonight and wouldn't have to share the hot tub with anyone else. No such luck. There was an older couple snuggling on one side of the spa. They were actually really cute together. But this would force me to have to sit close to Nathan. Not that I really minded.

I placed our towels down on the chairs that I knew had the killer view of the Las Vegas strip. My neighborhood was set just far enough off the strip to be away from it all, but close enough to still enjoy the views. Nathan quickly jumped in the spa, as if he needed to save us seats. At the same time, his eyes never left me. He really did like to watch. With a subtle giggle, I slowly dropped my cover-up. His normal golden eyes went dark with a look I'd yet to see. It was a look of desire, of hunger, and it sent a jolt of electricity to every part of my body.

Two could play at that game. I didn't get in the spa right away. As I sat down next to Nathan, I ever so slightly ran my leg up against his arm. He gently grabbed my right foot and began to slowly run his thumb up and down the pad of my foot. His skilled hands made my aching foot feel downright amazing. My other foot needed the same treatment, so I swung my legs around his strong, broad shoulders, resulting in both legs sitting on each side of his beautiful body. He continued to gently rub each one of my feet. My nails lightly scratched the back of Nathan's head as I ran my fingers through his thick hair. A low growl came from deep in his throat as we both continued to relax.

Not long after, the older couple must have sensed our

desire for a bit of privacy and quietly slipped away, although we barely noticed. "Come sit with me, Ryann," Nathan demanded, the edge of authority in his tone turning me on.

I carefully stood up, stepped into the hot tub and sat across from him. On purpose. "That's not with me, butterfly." He crooked his finger for me to come toward him. I stood up and slowly made my way to him. When I got within reach, Nathan grabbed ahold of my hips and pulled me up against his rock hard body. I softly sat down on his lap and put my arm around his neck to keep my balance. "Hi, beautiful."

"Hi," I whispered back. I could feel my heart wanting to jump out of my chest. I was sure Nathan could hear the thump of each powerful beat. He turned and looked me directly in the eyes, one hand around my waist and the other cupping my face.

"Ryann, I've been thinking about kissing you since the moment I laid eyes on you the night of your birthday. Tonight, I've been waiting to claim your lips as mine." With that, Nathan's mouth crashed onto mine. His tongue invaded my mouth with such fervor, I felt my toes curl as my fingers dug into his neck. Our tongues slowly wrestled, wanting to taste every bit of the other's. With each swirl, the hold he had around my waist was getting tighter and tighter. With a minor retreat, we both slowly pulled back, gently sucking on each other's lips. His slight five o'clock shadow, was gently scratching my face. Needing to breathe, I slowly pulled away and softly bit down on his bottom lip.

Not pulling my face too far away from his, I whispered,

"Wow." My brain couldn't seem to form any other words. We sat there for a minute just lost in our moment.

When I was able to regain my thoughts, I stood up and held my hand out for Nathan to follow. I placed a towel down on the double-wide lounger and lay down on my side looking out at the Vegas skyline. Nathan came up and spooned me from behind, leaned up on one elbow, and ran his other hand up and down my back.

"I found this spot one night when I needed to clear my head. This exact spot is the only place in the pool that has this view. I love to come here at night and escape," I told Nathan.

"Escape from what?" he asked.

I hesitated. "Life, I guess." He left my answer for what it was.

"It's the second most beautiful thing I've seen tonight," Nathan said as he kissed my neck. All I could do was moan and fall into his hold. It was so comfortable to lay there with him, losing track of time. We both drifted off to sleep, until security woke us as they were locking up for the night.

Nathan and I held hands as we quietly walked back to my condo. My mind started to race as we got closer to my door. What next? Do we kiss again? Do I ask him to stay? Do I have sex with him? As if he sensed my worry, he squeezed my hand and told me to stop thinking so much. It was like he knew me already.

As we got through the door, Nathan met my gaze. "I had a wonderful time tonight. Are we still on for tomorrow?"

I nodded. Of course we were. "Can you do early?" he asked.

"I think I may be able to fit you into my morning schedule. How early are we talking?"

"I'll pick you up at four-thirty," Nathan clearly stated. "It'll be worth it."

"Okay, at least let me make the coffee?"

"Deal." Nathan leaned in and kissed me once more. This kiss wasn't like the kiss in the hot tub. It was much shorter than the first; soft and tender. Our hands were laced together at our sides as he gently delved his tongue into my mouth like he couldn't get enough of the way I tasted.

"I'll see you in the morning, butterfly."

I could barely sleep after Nathan left, I was too wound up. That man and his tattoos made my body tingle in a way I didn't even think was possible. Every one of my lady bits screamed to have Nathan in my bed, yet my brain said slow down, hussy. This was the man who had the nerve to call you a MILF the other night and had still yet to explain it. I wanted a summer fling, but I wasn't interested in someone hurting me either. I wished I wasn't the type of person who had to have everything in my life lined up perfectly in front of me; every single damn duck in a row before I could move forward. But that's who I was.

When I let Roxy out at three forty-five the next morning, I could already feel the humidity in the hot desert air. There was a heavy cover of clouds and moisture that filled the early morning sky. I hoped the weather didn't have an effect on whatever Nathan's plans were. He didn't tell me what we were doing so I decided to just dress casual. I mean what could we really be doing at five in the morning? I threw on a cute pair of skinny jeans, my ripped MTV tank top, and my old black Chucks. I hated my hair in my face so I threw it up in loose ponytail and was ready to go. Being a kindergarten teacher had taught me to be really low maintenance.

I sent Nathan a text to let me know when he was close so I could meet him outside. I didn't want Roxy's inevitable barking to piss off all the neighbors.

Nathan: I'm there in 5 min

Me: Ok. I'll meet you in the driveway.

Nathan: Be safe butterfly. I'll be there shortly.

Not three minutes later, Nathan pulled up. "Ummm. You weren't texting and driving right?" I asked him as I climbed into the truck.

"Good morning to you too. And no I used Bluetooth, *Mom*," he said in his best smart ass voice.

"Sorry. Good morning, nuts," I laughed. I leaned over and kissed his scratchy cheek. "Where are we going?"

"You'll see."

The drive was quiet. I had never been good with surprises. I tended to overthink most situations. I reached over and turned on the radio to break the silence. *Confession* by Florida Georgia Line quietly started playing. The lyrics to that song had always ones I'd been able to get lost in.

Somewhere deep down in me, I knew there were so many confessions I had to make. Before I knew it, we pulled up in front of the Paris Casino.

"Why are we here?" I asked angrily. Confusion marred Nathan's features as he stared at me.

"Sunrise on the observation deck," he paused. "Ryann, are you okay?" Tears started to stream down my face.

"Take me home. Now. Please." It wasn't a request; it was a demand.

"Ryann, tell me what's wrong," Nathan pleaded.

"I can't do this. Just take me home!" I yelled at him. My anger had nothing to do with Nathan, but he was the only person there for me to take it out on. Of all the places in Las Vegas, Nathan could have taken me, he chose the one spot where I got married. Un-fucking believable.

When we pulled back in front of my condo, I sat there for a few seconds not really knowing what to say. Finally, I forced myself to meet his eyes, feeling guilty when I saw the concern in his. "I'm sorry, Nathan. I can't ever be what you need." With that, I slowly got out of the truck and shuffled into my house.

Nathan tried calling and texting me throughout the rest of the day. I just needed to be by myself and shut off everything except for the new season of Orange is the New Black. I felt stupid for freaking out on him like that. I should have just told him he took me to the exact spot where I married my jerk of an ex. But in that moment, I was so pissed off and hurt that I just needed to be away from him. Away from that memory.

Tuesday and Wednesday, I went to work and avoided the VIP booths at all costs. I knew that's where the money was but I just couldn't bring myself to see Nathan. Rose told me he was there both nights. I figured Ashlynn would just give him his usual massages and all would go back to the way it was before. But the girls said he just sat there by himself. It was definitely a sad situation, according to them.

Thursday night came, and I couldn't avoid the booths any longer. G was back in town for the week and he wanted us to "hang out" according to Jade. I hated when people do air quotes. What the hell does "hang out" really mean then? Did it matter? I *wanted* to experience reckless abandon this summer. There was this thing with Nathan. But Nathan was here in Vegas, where I lived. Where I taught. It was all too real. G goes back to New England in August for training. He would be a hot summer fling. *I mean have you seen his body?*

After meeting G at *The Cave* the first time, I went home and Googled him to find out what he was really all about. He was known for being the NFL playboy. He broke women's hearts as often as he broke his opponents' noses. He was a strip club frequenter and liked to date and show his women off. But at the same time, women gushed about him, how he had a big heart and cuddled like a teddy bear. When it came to G here at the club, I had a job to do. I knew it would be a whole different ball game if I saw him outside of the club on my own time. If that's what "hang out" meant. I just didn't think I could be the kind of girl G would expect me to be. *Ugh,*

I'm rambling again.

I stopped by the main bar to grab a drink from Rose. As I sat there with her, I glanced up at the VIP booths and could see Nathan looking directly at us. *Shit.* I knew he deserved an explanation. I had no idea why I was afraid to give it to him. Yes, I did. I really liked him. I couldn't risk some strip club regular finding out what my real job is. And I didn't want to face rejection again when he found that I could never give him a family. Nope not worth it.

I grabbed my drink and sauntered my ass up to G in his booth right next to Nathan's. "Back so soon, big guy?" I asked as I sat down next to him.

"When you look this damn good, baby girl, how could I not?" he growled, waving his hands in front of my body.

"I was hoping I'd see you tonight, so I decided to wear something extra sexy," I whispered back. Completely not true, but this job was all about playing into our customers. And G was just another customer. Tonight I wore a black and pink lace lingerie set. It was absolutely gorgeous. It was one of those pieces that covered your stomach but had open sides and a back. My boobs and crotch were only covered by a thin piece of black lace. It unsnapped behind the neck giving my girls easy release when it was time. "Let's go someplace more private," I told him.

Knowing damn well I had to walk by Nathan's booth, I took G by the hand and led him into the private rooms. I needed Nathan to see this. If I pissed him off bad enough, he'd stop watching me and neither one us would get hurt by the situation. But how far was I willing to go with G to make that happen?

When we got to the empty room, G sat down and roughly pulled me down on his lap. This man was more than double my size, there's no possibility I could pull away even if I wanted to. The problem was, I didn't think I wanted to. The women on the internet were right, G was like a giant teddy bear.

"You really are a beautiful lady, Vaughn," G said as he pushed a fallen hair behind my ear. Ah, there's that name again. Vaughn. The fake me. Each time G saw me I had on my brown wig, and different color eyes. I guess it was so dark in the club he didn't notice.

"Why, thank you. You're not too bad yourself there, big boy," I teased as I batted my long fake eyelashes at him.

"Dance for me, Vaughn," he said in his drawn out ultra-sexy voice. Damn accents.

"Of course." I played *Nice and Slow* by Usher on the speakers. I took a few steps back so he could see all of my body, and started slowly moving in front of him. Dancing is all about the suggestive movements and eye contact. And with G, none of it was hard. I untied the ribbon that held my top together down the center I started rubbing my nipples until they were fully erect. Turning myself around, I backed up until I was sitting directly on his lap. "Untie me, G."

He did as I told him to, also making sure he ran his massive hands directly down my side, over my hips and left them there. My top fell to the floor. Slowly, I raised my arms and held my hair up, exposing my entire backside as I grinded my hips into his ever growing erection. As I leaned all the way into him, I rested my head on his shoulder, and exposed my tits to him. His body felt so strong, it encouraged me to keep going when I heard the sultry moan escape from his throat.

There was a moment of quiet when the song ended. "Vaughn, would you be willing to take it all off for me tonight?" G asked. "I really want to see all of this beautiful body in front of me."

I knew G had a reputation for expecting more from the girls, so what exactly did he want from me? As *Pour it Up* by Rhianna came on, it reminded me that this was all about the money, but I still wouldn't compromise my limits.

"One condition. I will dance completely nude, but hands off big guy," I said sternly. G nodded. With that, I began to slowly take off the lace bottoms I still had on, moving my body with the rhythm of the song. Rocking my hips back and forth, I slowly cupped my own breasts. I moved closer to him, and could see the pure lust in his eyes. I could now understand how women could get swept up by him. He was fine as hell. After the other night with Nathan, and now tonight dancing again for G, the ache that was forming between my legs screamed to push his large erection in front of me, deep into my core. It had been too long since I'd felt the touch of a man.

I have no idea what the next song was, but G requested three songs, so I kept dancing. Even completely nude, there was something about him that made me feel comfortable. Moving onto G's lap, I rubbed my breasts close enough to his face that I felt his warm breath against my nipples. I could only imagine that he'd be an awesome fuck. I bet Nathan would be an awesome fuck as well. I bet these two men fucking me together would be fantastic. Holy shit, where did that come from?

Knowing the song was coming to an end, I was going to make damn sure I had control of my own release tonight. I shifted myself on G's lap, again with my back towards him, but this time we were both facing the mirrors. I used one hand to pinch my right nipple and used the other hand to gently rub my clit. I continued to go faster and harder until I felt the orgasm creeping through every inch of my body. My eyes popped open and looked directly into G's as I gave myself my first orgasm in weeks. *Holy freaking hotness...*

"Damn, baby girl," he growled.

As I was changing and cleaning up for the night, Vanessa came in and handed me an envelope. "What's this?" I asked. She shrugged her shoulders and walked out. Jade and Bree were by my side in an instant, like moths to a flame, waiting for me to open the envelope. They both knew that I spent the evening in a private room with G. I stepped away, so I could look at whatever this was first. I pulled out the note.

Vaughn,

You rocked my world tonight, baby girl.

I am in town for a couple weeks.

Let me take you to dinner.

I'll be in touch soon.

RG

Along with the note, he attached three thousand dollars. *Holy shitballs*! I wasn't sure if I should've been ecstatic or pissed off. Why was I confused about this? I danced for a rich man and he tipped me well. But now what? I was not a prostitute. I showed the girls the note, and of course being the two youngest of all of us are here, they were completely jealous. I needed to give Vanessa a call for some advice

"I can't believe G tipped you three grand, Vaughn," Bree shouted as we bounced down the hall to our cars.

"Yeah, it was a crazy night tonight," I said.

Out of nowhere, Nathan appeared in the hallway and stood in front of us. "Did I hear that fucking right? G tipped you three grand, Vaughn?" I could see the anger in his eyes and heard it in his voice. "I should have listened to my instincts. You are no different than the rest of them. You bitches are all the same," Nathan almost snarled at us, before storming out the back door.

"What the fuck was that all about?" Damon came out of his office; furious.

"I have no idea, Mr. White," Bree answered. "Vaughn and I were discussing her tip from a VIP tonight and Mr. Sims came unglued."

I stood there stunned. What the hell was Nathan's

problem? I understood he was pissed off at me, but I wouldn't let him put my job in jeopardy. I needed the money. G's tip just paid three months' rent for me. "I will fix it, Mr. White. Sorry."

I ran out the door after Nathan but he was already long gone. I pulled out my phone and brought up his number.

Me: WTF Nathan?? Meet me at my house in 20 minutes. We need to talk.

I didn't hear back from Nathan, so I had no idea if he was coming over or if he even got my message. But when he pulled up an hour later, I assumed he was trying to gain the upper hand by showing up when he wanted to. It was after three in the morning, and the last thing I wanted to do was cause any kind of disturbance in my complex. I stood there in the doorway as he walked up in an effort to keep Roxy from barking. I could smell the beer on him as he stood on my front porch waiting for me to invite him in.

"Have you been drinking?" I asked.

"Why yes, *Mother*! Am I in trouble?" Nathan sneered in the same smart ass tone he'd used before.

"What the hell, Nathan? Come inside, please." He followed me and I grabbed us some water before we both sat on the couch. He'd been drinking but he wasn't drunk.

"Did you fuck G?" Nathan bold faced asked me.

"No."

"Did you suck his dick?" I could see the hurt and anger mixed in his face.

"Nathan." I frowned. "No."

"Then why in the fuck would G tip you three grand? Tell me truth Ryann," Nathan said flatly.

Ouch. He used my real name. Well, why wouldn't he. I hoped that's not who Nathan thinks of me as. "I don't know. He likes me I guess."

"Bullshit, Ryann!" he yelled. This caused Roxy to look up to see if I needed protection.

"Fine!" I yelled back. "I danced nude for him. Is that what you wanted to fucking hear? This is my job, Nathan. That tip tonight paid my rent for three fucking months. You have no idea what that kind of money means to someone like me. I don't make a ton of fucking money with the drop of the fucking cards. And why the fuck do you even care?" Damn, I was crying again. Why did this man always make me cry?

"Because I care about you Ryann," Nathan admitted as he wiped the tears off my cheek.

Kiss Me Slowly

How much more could I question Ryann about G? I knew this was her job, I mean damn it was my club. But I knew his reputation. G and his buddies' faces had been plastered all over the tabloids regarding his quick and scandalous relationships with women. That was the last thing I wanted for Ryann. She's new to this business, but she can't be that naive. She seemed like the type of woman that if I were to tell her something she would do the exact opposite.

"Truth?" Ryann nodded to my question. "I was jealous of G. I like you, Ryann. I understand that this is your job. But not with G, in a room where I can't see you."

"Truth?" she asked me. Of course I nodded and softly took her hand. "I like you too, Nathan. But I need this job." She took a deep breath, choosing her next words carefully. "My life has been in a constant tail spin since my divorce. Yeah, I'm divorced. You are the first guy I've even talked to, no less kissed, since my ex. The other morning, you took me to the same spot I got married."

"Fuck me. Really? Oh, butterfly, I'm so sorry. I had no idea," I said as I pulled Ryann into my lap. "I would have never..." She stopped me by gently placing her lips on mine.

"Shhh... I never said anything. My shitty marriage is

something I choose not to talk about. There's no way you could have known anything. I'm sorry for ruining our first date."

I delicately kissed her nose. "That wasn't our first date. When I take you out on a date it will be a night you will never forget. We've all been in bad relationships that leave us with memories that haunt us. Trust me, I understand."

"Nathan?" Ryann softy said my name. Just hearing her say my name made my dick jump in my shorts. Her voice was so soft and sexy.

"Yeah?"

"Take me to bed or loose me forever," she giggled.

"Did you just flippin' quote *Top Gun*?" I asked.

"Hell yes! Best movie ever!" Her laugh had now become a belly laugh; she almost fell off my lap.

I think she was deliriously tired. "C'mon. Let's get you to bed, silly girl." I scooped her up in my arms and carried her to her room. I could see the droopiness in her eyes.

"I need a shower," she informed me.

I carried Ryann into the bathroom and gently sat her down on the oversized bench. Walking over to the shower, I started the water for her. *Should I give her privacy? Should I get in with her?* My mind raced like I was a damn chick or something. What the fuck was wrong with me?

"I'll give you some privacy, butterfly," I regretfully said, as I turned to walk out.

"Thanks. Nathan? Will you be here when I get out?"

"Do you want me to be?" Ryann looked me right in the eye and nodded. "Then there's no place else I'd rather be." I smiled at her and shut the door.

Heading into the kitchen, I switched on the Keurig and made us some hot tea to unwind from our night. I threw Roxy on her leash and took her for a quick walk out to my truck, and grabbed a pair of sweats from my gym bag. Damn, this all felt so normal. When I came back in I could hear the shower was still going so I knew I had a few more minutes.

I changed, brought the tea to her room, and laid down on what I hoped wasn't her side of the bed. I grabbed my phone and started scrolling my calendar to begin planning my visit with Ella in the next few weeks. When Ryann walked out of the bathroom, my jaw all but hit the ground. The woman was a natural fucking beauty. Her blonde hair and brown eyes shined, especially when she wasn't covered up with all that stage makeup. Her curves were natural and her body was tight. I could see even through the pajama shirt she had on. I couldn't wait to sink my cock deep into that voluptuous ass, but that would have to wait. Because even as beautiful as she was, I sensed a deep nervousness within her.

"I hope this is okay with you? I can go share the couch again with Roxy," I laughed. I really hoped my asshole behavior earlier wouldn't get me kicked out of her bed. She didn't deserve how I'd treated her. All I wanted to do was be close to her, helping both of us relax from a couple of shitty days.

"It's perfect," Ryann said as she climbed into bed next to me and grabbed her tea. "Thanks for the tea… and for coming over tonight…I'm sor—"

"Shhh," I interrupted her, and put my lips on hers. I knew she was going to apologize for things that just didn't require any apologizing for. "No apologies. Do you know what I'm sorry really means?" I asked. She shook her head. "It means you're never going to do it again. Are you going to make me jealous and act like an idiot again? Probably." I could start to see her smile come out. "So neither one of us can apologize for these things. Instead we just kiss and makeup."

With that, I took the coffee mug from her hand and placed it on the nightstand. I stood up and moved around to the other side of the bed, and swiftly crawled on top of my girl. Yeah, she was mine. I was going to make sure she knew it very soon. I placed a gentle kiss directly behind her ear and more down her neck. I loved the soft moans Ryann made when I kissed her. Her fingers began to gently rub my sides. When a girl ran her nails up and down my sides, it was my fucking kryptonite. I was putty in her damn hands and I was sure she could feel my cock getting bigger against her leg. She moved her hands down and started playing with the elastic band on my pants.

"You're playing with fire there," I whispered onto her lips. I propped myself up on my elbows and looked at her. "Ryann, I cannot wait to kiss every inch of your gorgeous body and see if the rest of you tastes as good as your lips. I can't stop thinking about burying my cock deep inside your warmth while you scream only my name." I watched her brown eyes grow dark with desire. "But not tonight. I want the night I claim you as mine to be something you never forget." I leaned over and kissed those luscious pink lips that had been screaming at me to devour them. I couldn't help myself from thinking that she had already been naked for G tonight. When I make my butterfly soar it will be a night shared only by the two of us.

Pulling her body close to mine, she laid her head on my chest and sprawled one leg over both of my legs. Her fingers slowly rubbed my chest, and I quickly got lost in the fresh scent of her coconut hair. It didn't take long for both of us to fall asleep.

***

"Mmmm...Ryann...toes in the morning...that's some kinky shit," I mumbled half asleep with barely open eyes. I'd been dreaming about Ryann and I sitting poolside at the Bellagio after I won a tournament tickling our toes in the water.

"Hey, sleepy head. You're awake," Ryann said as she appeared in the doorway.

If Ryann was at the door, who was licking my toes? "Ahhh! Roxy!" I yelled and pulled my legs up. Ryann burst out laughing.

"I warned you. Get up. I made Rose's banana pancakes."

"Yum. If it came from Rose, then I know it tastes good."

"Well, thanks," Ryann huffed.

"That's not what I meant. I'm sure you made it with more love." Oh shit? Did I just say that? I got up and followed her into the kitchen. Embarrassed about what I said, I gave her a kiss on the cheek and sat down on the stool behind the counter. I did love to watch this woman. Maybe I was the creepy, stalker guy.

"Any plans for today?" Ryann asked as she made our plates.

"I need to go talk to Damon. Last night was not cool. That was an "I'm sorry" moment. I will not act like that again. What are your plans?" I returned the question.

"Every Friday during summer vacation Ali, Rose's daughter, and I have a standing lunch date. We go eat, and then go to the movies, shopping or something fun like that. Today we're bathing suit shopping, because Auntie Ry buys the cool stuff. What can I say, I'm a pushover for that one," she smiled as she talked about Ali. It made me miss my J-Ella Bean even more.

"One day you will make a beautiful mother, Ryann," I told her. And with that her sparkle was gone. She abruptly turned and started clearing our plates. What the hell did I say now?

"Will I see you at *The Cave* tonight?" she asked, her voice curt.

"I was planning on it. Everything alright, butterfly?" I asked as I walked up and put my arms around her waist. "Did

I say something to upset you?"

"No…I'm fine…I just didn't realize the time. Can we talk later?"

Shit. She said fine. It's not fine, but I could tell it wasn't something to push. I pulled Ryann close to me and held her for a minute and gently kissed the top of her head. "Whenever you're ready, beautiful. I'll see you tonight."

Grabbing my bag, I left Ryann's almost on a mission. I had a lot of shit I needed to sort out and plan if everything was to work out right. My first stop was the club. I acted like a douche and I didn't need to bring that around work with our VIPs.

Later on in that same afternoon, I trudged into Damon's office. "Hey," I greeted him.

"Oh, well hello. Sir Fucking Crazy Ass Nut Sackage," he almost yelled at me. "What the fuck, dude? What happened last night with you? G brings in a lot of money and he likes Vaughn. Deal with it."

"Yeah, well, I get it. I'm sorry for acting like a dick last night. But you know as well as I do that Ryann is not just another dancer," I said sternly. I could see the look on his face change. "I know she's only here because her show is on hiatus and needs the money. All I can say is that I like her. After Jordyn, I wanted to keep my distance from any dancers. But I can't with her."

"Fine, bro. I get it. What do you want from me?" he asked.

"Keep her away from G!"

"You know I can't do that. That's up to her. But you can," he said with a sneaky smile. "Oh, look. Vaughn's schedule just happens to be free tonight. Not anymore."

"Thanks, bud. I'll see you tonight," I left and headed to the parking lot. Climbing in my truck, I grabbed my phone and sent a text to Vanessa.

Me: Hey girl—I need your help please.

Vanessa: Of course. What can I do?

Me: Let Vaughn know she was booked by a VIP with a special request. All black leather.

There was no reason for the leather except is was fucking hot. The way the material hugged a woman's body drove me nuts. The thought of Ryann tucked into a tight skirt caused my dick to perk up.

Vanessa: Really? Sounds hot.

Me: It will be. And if all goes well, she won't be in tomorrow night.

Vanessa: What's going on Nathan?

I left that text unanswered. Just one more text before I am off to run some errands and make sure Ryann doesn't have any excuses.

Me: Hi butterfly. I hope you are enjoying shopping with Ali. Question—Any plans for your days off?

Ryann: Nothing too much. Why? What's up?

Me: I have a 3 day tournament in Laughlin. I would love it if you would join me.

No response. I knew I would get my answer from her that night.

I pulled up the club at about nine-thirty in my rented red Mustang. I didn't want to drive my own car, if Ryann saw it she'd know I was there. I wanted to surprise her. Plus, I wanted to show her what some real power behind the wheel felt like. I booked a private room for the evening requesting only Vaughn—the VIP that requested her all damn evening. *Fuck...what do I call her at the club?* I didn't want to look at her as Vaughn Haley. That's not who she was to me. But I knew when we were at *The Cave* she didn't want to be called Ryann. Easy enough to stick with just calling her my butterfly.

I called Rose before the evening began and asked her to set up the room with a bottle of vodka and Jack Daniels so that we wouldn't be disturbed for the next few hours. I had no intention of having her strip for me tonight, but I also didn't want her stripping for anyone else until we figured "us" out. Hell, I had the money to cover whatever her tips would have been that night. I just wanted to spend time with her and hopefully convince her to spend the weekend with me.

The lights were down low when Ryann entered, preventing her from seeing my face, but I sure as hell could see her. She was wearing a black leather bra, a tight leather mini skirt and thigh-high heeled leather boots. Holy fuck, my dick instantly got hard. She had on a black wig, giving my

121

changing butterfly an almost dominatrix look. I needed to ask her to wear this outfit for me at home.

"Mr. Sackage?" she asked, coming farther into the room. *Fucking Damon*. That's what I get for letting him sign me up for the room after I caused a scene last night.

"Please, call me by first name," I told her.

"Okay. Newt. Really? Newt Sackage?" Ryann flipped on the lights and fuck if I didn't get the hottest view I ever fucking saw. The back of her leather skirt was connected only by three belt buckles. Nothing else there but her bare, perfectly round ass. I was dying to sink my fingers into her tanned flesh. She spun back and caught me almost drooling at the sight of her. "Nathan. What's going on?"

"I wanted to spend an evening with you," I grabbed her hand and pulled her toward me.

"I'm flattered. I am, but I was counting on the extra money," she said, disappointed.

"The money? Or G?" I demanded. "I'll pay you if that's what you want." Crap. That's not how I meant for that to sound. I'm not sure how I meant for it to sound but not like that.

"I'm not a fucking hooker, Nathan. I don't sleep with my clients," she spat. Damn, I upset her again.

"Ryann, that's not what I meant and you know it. I told you I was jealous. I booked the time with you tonight so G couldn't. And if that means paying you VIP tips, baby, I will."

Her expression softened. She sat her naked ass down

directly on my lap, and ran her fingers through the back of my hair. "Nathan, c'mon now. G's hot and all," she giggled. "But remember who I shared my bed with last night." She kissed me softly right along my jawline. "G is a nice guy, but he's part of my job. You're my friend."

"Ouch. Friend zone, huh?" I ran my hands along her bare thighs.

"You know what I meant nuts," she playfully slapped my chest.

"Come away with me this weekend." I prepared myself for her excuses.

"I have to work tomorrow."

"Vanessa said she'd cover your shift."

"I don't have anyone to watch Roxy and I can't leave her alone all weekend."

Thought of this one too. "Does Roxy like other dogs?"

Ryann nodded. "Usually," she answered.

"Then it's handled, she can stay at my house with my house sitter. Just one last thing," I said to her.

"And what is that?" Ryann asked cuddling up closer.

"You to say yes, beautiful."

"Well, since you have it all covered, Nathan, how could I say no? Yes, I will go with you this weekend," Ryann agreed.

She leisurely moved and straddled my lap, pressing herself straight down on my rock hard erection. "I have a few more hours left on my shift and it seems like I'm booked with a very important person. I need to make sure Mr. Sackage gets the full experience here at *The Cave*," Ryann whispered as she leaned over me to turn on the music. I inhaled every part of her body as she pressed herself close against me.

"If your body is this close to me, I can't control myself from not touching you. I need to have you naked next to me. And trust me I will have you," I practically growled with desire. "Not here. Let's start our time away now."

"Nathan, I can't leave early," Ryann shrieked.

"Is it the money? I told you I would cover your tips tonight." I knew she didn't like the idea of taking money from me, but I'm the one who booked her, and I booked her until closing.

"No. After the scene with you last night, I don't want to tell the owner that I'm going home early with a client," Ryann said, completely frustrated.

Is that how she still thought of me? As a friend? As a client? I needed to take control of this situation. Now. "I'm more than a client, butterfly. The owner says you're leaving with him. Let's go," I said with more authority in my voice than I've used before. The look in her eye told me she wasn't going to question what I told her to do.

We stood up, and I escorted her out of the room with my hand on her hip the entire time. I walked behind Ryann at all times making sure that I was the only one who could see her succulent ass. An ass which continued to tempt me in a way that I no longer wanted to control. We went straight to the back, grabbed her purse and left. On Friday nights, I knew Ryann drove with Rose to work so we wouldn't have to worry about her car. She stopped, looked around, and had no idea where to go next when she didn't see my truck in the parking lot.

"I'm going to show you some real power this weekend, beautiful," I said as I opened the door to the Mustang for her. Ryann just shook her head, laughed and crawled in. We drove to her condo first so that she could pack a bag for the weekend, and pack up Roxy to bring her to my place. I knew this made her a bit nervous at first, until she saw my oversized yard and dog run that I had custom built for Cheech.

"That's quite a setup you have here, nuts. I'm assuming by the size of the run here your dog is quite active."

"Come inside. You can meet him and the sitter, Molly." When we walked through the door, Cheech didn't even look up from Molly scratching his belly. The drool just continued to ruin my couch. I actually heard Ryann chuckle when she first saw my dog.

"Yeah, I don't think he needs anything more than the couch," she laughed. I introduced all the dogs and humans and everyone seemed to be comfortable with one another. Excellent, we were set to begin the two-hour drive to Laughlin. By driving, I hoped that we could talk and start getting to know each other more.

I gave Ryann some time to settle in and get comfortable on our drive before we started those conversations.

She broke the ice. "Okay, Mr. Owner. Want to explain that one please?"

"Yesterday, I said we all come with baggage. Let me tell you about mine," I sighed. I started by telling her about Damon and Isabell and how I then became part owner of *The Cave* and how that led me to meet Jordyn. I explained how our relationship was rocky and that we moved to San Diego for her to go to nursing school and that we broke up because she cheated on me with another dancer from the club. I left out Ella. I never once thought of her as baggage and I figured it was a conversation for another time.

Ryann told me about her ex-husband, Lucas. They'd had a great relationship until they didn't. Basically one day, he just changed his mind and left. I had a feeling there was more to the story but I didn't want to push her, especially before our weekend together.

I was playing in a three-day quarter million-dollar poker tournament. They could be boring twelve hour days, but the payoff could be big if I finished in the top twenty-five. The only payoff I truly cared about this weekend was with my butterfly.

Into You

I felt like my brain was all discombobulated, like I was on a damn roller coaster of emotions. After a great couple of nights getting to know Nathan, we'd had that awful morning at the Paris Hotel. Yet that had nothing to do with him. But it made me realize that I was not ready to do this dating thing yet. And now my new job, one VIP in particular, was already causing Nathan and me to argue. But argue for a good reason, I mean he was jealous of G—Ah— G. Richard Grovanski, NFL playboy. The man tipped me enough to pay three months of rent and wanted to take me out to dinner. That man made me feel sexy as hell, but he was a client, and I was beginning to learn his reputation with women.

On my way to pick up Ali, I called Vanessa. "Hey, girl. Got a minute?"

"Hey, teach. Sure do, what's up?" she asked.

"So long story short. Nathan and I have been flirting...and arguing back and forth for a couple weeks now. Last night we had a long talk and we admitted we have feelings for each other. But this was only after he heard I spent another evening with G and received a three thousand dollar tip," I explained to her.

"Holy shit. Is that what was in the envelope?"

"Yes." I also told her about how he wrote me note, asking me out to dinner. "I have no idea what the hell to think. Both guys are clients, and I remember what Ashlynn said about it all getting messy. Nathan's a regular, G's famous. What the hell do I do?"

"Girl, there's no set rule about dating clients, but think about where this all will lead in the end. There's a world beyond *The Cave*, don't get caught up in all of this. Here's what I will say. Nathan is one of my best friends. He's a good guy. G is hot but has reputation with the ladies. Think carefully before doing anything. Oh and on a totally different note. You've been booked by a VIP tonight that requested you in all black leather."

"Really? Who?"

"I don't know. I wasn't told," Vanessa explained.

"Hmmm. Okay. I can make it work. Thanks for listening. Let's get together on Sunday," I suggested.

"I...ummm...might be busy. I'll see you tonight."She hung up abruptly.

What was Vanessa's change in attitude about? It was like she didn't want to tell me something. I'd have to talk to her tonight. Today was all about Ali. Not having kids of my own made me love these times I got to spend with her even more. There's something fun about being the cool auntie. Plus, it gave me a chance to just forget the drama and get some retail therapy in. Today our plans were lunch and the mall.

As much as I tried to focus on Ali, all day my mind kept wandering to my VIP request that night. I haven't been at the club long enough to have regular requests, so this was a bit odd. I assumed it was G. I mean who else would it be? Would he expect more? Would I make another three grand? Should I go out with him? Does that make me a prostitute? Damn, I needed to work on my mind running wild.

That evening, I found the sexiest leather get-up I could and got ready for another night of half-naked dancing. Whoever it is, I knew my limits and would not compromise that for any amount of money. But I definitely wouldn't mind dancing for G again. There was something about him that made me feel like a sexy woman. I needed that right now. Almost as much as I needed the money. Not that Nathan didn't make me feel sexy, but G was different. I checked the VIP names and saw it was booked under the name Newt Sackage. Really? I understood using a name to not get identified, but grow up gentlemen.

Before I started my evening, I scanned the parking lot to see if Nathan's truck was parked out there. Nothing. No Harley either. That morning he'd once again thrown me for a loop when he said I would be a good mother someday. I knew I had to tell him, but when? Part of me was hoping Nathan was my VIP tonight, and yet another part of me wanted it to be G. Either way, I looked hot and I was going to dance my ass off for whoever paid to be with me. I just hoped it wasn't the dirty, old man from my first week, but I highly doubted he was a VIP.

I wasn't sure how I felt when I switched on the lights and saw Nathan sitting there. The way he stared at me, with such desire, such lust, sent a shiver all the way up my spine. I was definitely falling for him and for that same reason I was disappointed. The last time I was requested in a private room, I made big money. Money that would pay three months' worth of rent. Something about taking money from Nathan felt completely wrong. I wasn't there to fall for a guy, I was there to make some cash.

After some arguing and persuading, Nathan convinced me to go to Laughlin with him for a few days. He was playing in a poker tournament and I figured the time away would be a nice break. There was only about a month left before my summer vacation was over and I had to go back to my everyday life. He told me I could come and watch him play, but I felt like me being there would be a distraction for him. I'd much rather spend my days lying by the pool and reading, or shopping if I had the money.

On the drive to the casino, Nathan told me about being a silent owner of *The Cave* and his ex-girlfriend, Jordyn. It now made sense now why he had this constant hot and cold attitude towards me. He said dating a dancer was something he would never do again. What did it mean for us? I had the urge right there to tell him I was really a broke ass teacher and only started dancing so I didn't have to move home with my mother and her nudist boyfriend. But the thought of being honest terrified me. The risk was still just too big. I did tell Nathan about my divorce, yet not the complete truth on why. After the rejection I had felt from what happened, I wasn't ready to share my brokenness with any other man. Damn, I really hated not being honest.

We checked into our suite a little before two in the morning, and we were both exhausted. He had to be in the poker room by eight in the morning, so I knew he needed to get to sleep. I wasn't going to be the reason Nathan wasn't on his game for the tournament. I couldn't even imagine playing for something where first prize was over a hundred thousand dollars. Poker was Nathan's job and I wasn't there to distract his concentration in any way.

"What's wrong? You've been too quiet since we got here," he commented as we entered our room.

"Nothing, honey. I promise. I was just thinking about how I don't want to be a distraction for you here at this tournament," I answered.

Nathan laced his hands around my waste. "Did you just call me honey?"

Shit. "Yeah, I did," I admitted, embarrassed. I tried to wiggle out of Nathan's hold but he wasn't letting me go.

"Don't you try and get away from me, butterfly," he whispered as he pulled me into a tighter hold against his body. "You're so cute when you get embarrassed," he kissed my nose. "Your cheeks turn the prettiest shade of pink when you blush," he kissed both of my cheeks.

"You may call me honey or any other name you want as long it comes from these sweet lips," his passionate kiss caused my entire body to break out in goosebumps. I gasped for breath when Nathan pulled away from me. "So, I didn't want to assume anything about the sleeping arrangements. I got us a two-bedroom suite."

"You really are a gentleman aren't you?" I asked.

"Ryann, I want to sleep next you. I want to hold you and watch you relax in my arms. But I'm not going to push you into anything you aren't ready for," he whispered against my lips.

He made me nervous. Nervous in such a good way. He said all the right things just when I needed him to. I was definitely excited for what the weekend could entail for us. There was no way in hell I was going to sleep in a separate room. *Reckless abandon it was.*

"C'mon," I grabbed his hand and led him into the larger of the two bedrooms and closed the door behind us.

I woke up the next morning to a note:

Good Morning butterfly,

Today I want you to relax.

You have a spa appointment at 11. Enjoy baby.

Here is your tip for last night. Don't say no.

Go shopping and buy yourself something pretty.

Meet me at the steakhouse at 8pm.

Nathan

This man almost seemed to be good to be true, but at the moment I was willing to take what he was giving me. I needed this. I deserved this. I was enjoying Nathan. When I got to the spa, I felt like a kid in a candy store when I found out I was to pick any of the packages that I desired. It truly was a moment a girl dreamt of. I chose a massage, a facial, and a complete nail package. It was one of those days that made you feel like a princess.

As I was laying there getting my massage, I realized that I didn't want to share Nathan. I would text him my change of plans. Hopefully he would get a text. They had to have some kind of breaks right?

Me: Hi honey. Thank you for my spa day. This place is great. Change of plans. See you tonight in our suite at 8. Xoxo

Now time to go shopping and make what will be our first date a memorable night. I first went to a store that sold bubble bath and candles. If I was going to create the ambiance, might as well make it my dream night. What did I hear the kids say nowadays, *yolo*. Right, you only live once. So why not make my night with Nathan what I wanted it to be. Cliché, but who gave a shit right?

Passing by a lingerie store, I had to go in. I didn't want to wear the same pieces with Nathan as I did to the club. Well unless it's something he requested. I had a feeling the leather get-up might be coming home soon. As I skimmed through all the racks, I found a navy blue butterfly bra and panty set. It was perfect to go under the loose black dress I planned on wearing. Walking out of the store, I received a text message alert.

Nathan: I'm glad you enjoyed yourself. Your plans sound perfect. See you at 7. I won't be able to hold out until 8.

Me: Can't wait.

That only gave me three hours to get ready, but I easily pulled it off with a little bit of teacher time management: an hour for my bath, an hour for myself, and an hour for our room. Definitely in my doable range. Even if this was only a summer fling, I wanted it to be a time that I would not forget. A time to remind myself, broken or not, I could be a sexy woman.

For me, music had always been everything. I was the type of person that has a song for every moment. When I was a little girl, my dad would always put the oversized headphones on my ears and we would rock out together to the beat of the music. As I got older, music became about the lyrics for me. It was like getting lost in a short story, some much better than others. I knew tonight would be a mix of all those playlists I've spent hours making, to remember that night. Again, cliché... but that's who I was.

Crawling into the amazing tub in our room, I hit my go to escape playlist on my iPod. I grabbed my glass of wine and my Kindle, knowing I had just under an hour to get lost in my latest book of a woman feeling torn between her two great loves. With every word I read, I became more and more distracted. I was definitely feeling torn between Nathan and G. Not that I loved either one of these men by any means, but feeling wanted by two men was something new to me. I knew with Nathan I felt sexy and safe. There was something so real about him, and that scared the hell out of me. With G, it was a different kind of sexy, it was a lustful sexy. I knew anything with him would be a one-time fantasy. I would just be another notch on his belt, but damn, it would be fun. Time to put G out of my head, this weekend was about Nathan.

I spent the next couple hours getting the room and myself ready. I changed the reservations at the steakhouse to be delivered and set up on the patio in our suite. We had a beautiful view which overlooked the river, so why not take advantage of it. I set up the room with a few candles and some soft music. I wanted to make the evening romantic but sexy. Nathan preferred my natural blonde hair and brown eyes to anything else I could put on. So I curled my hair, covered my body in my coconut lotion he seemed to like so much, and put on just enough makeup to make me feel pretty.

At precisely seven o'clock, Nathan walked through the door. I was sitting on the patio waiting for him, and couldn't help but stare as he walked towards me. He had on loose fitting jeans that hung perfectly around his well sculpted hips, a fitted black t-shirt that perfectly showed off his tattoos, and a red hat which brought out the amazing gold in his eyes. "Hey, handsome. Good day?" I asked, as I stood up to greet him.

"Actually, no," he answered as he pulled me into his warm embrace.

"See, I told you I shouldn't have come," I whined as I went to pull away from him.

"Don't you pull away from me," he laughed. "My poker game was fine. I did really well today."

"So...why was it a bad day?" I asked.

"Because every time I thought about what you were doing up here I would get a fucking hard on at the table."

I couldn't help but bust out laughing. "It was not funny," he pouted.

I put both my hands on his chest and started to push away. "Go take a shower, dinner will be here in twenty minutes," I told him.

He pulled me in tighter. "Oh please tell me I get to start with dessert," he whispered into my ear, his hands moving down to my ass. He kissed me in a way that made me want to just say screw dinner, but I wanted tonight to last.

"Later, nuts. Go clean up," I instructed as I pushed him off to the shower.

Half an hour later, we were eating dinner, discussing our day. I knew nothing about the world of professional poker, so listening to him talk about what he did all day was fascinating. Nathan explained that you could be the top rated guy out there, but if you weren't getting the cards you could be done the first day. Poker was definitely a mix between skill and luck. I guess he'd done fairly well today, considering he was still playing.

After we had both finished eating, I got up and went over and sat in Nathan's lap. There was something about him that I found completely irresistible. "Are you ready for dessert now?" I asked as I started running my newly manicured nails up and down his chest.

"Beautiful, I have been waiting on dessert since you sent me that text this afternoon," he quietly said as he began to twist the end of my curls with his fingers.

"Let's go inside. I have something for you," I whispered as I stood and pulled him inside with me. I sat him down in the chair in the middle of the room and then skipped to the perfect song I found to give him what I owed him.

Ariana Grande may be a bit cheesy for the moment, but as I said before, I was a lyrics girl. Plus, I wanted to keep things sexy and fun and not have it all get too serious. As soon as the beat began to play, I moved my hips along with the music and slowly inched myself closer to where Nathan was sitting. I loved watching the color of his hazel eyes deepen when he watched me dance. Moving behind where he was sitting, I reached down, grabbed the ends of his shirt and pulled it right off his body. This was our dance and I was going to enjoy it just as much as he was going to.

Sliding my body back around, so I was face to face with him, I couldn't help but kiss his sexy lips. My insides burned the moment I ran my fingers across his rock hard abs. Running my fingers across his rock hard abs, made my insides burn. He had a way of turning me on by just looking in my direction. Nathan quickly grabbed the bottom of my dress and pulled it over my head. I felt his erection starting to grow when he saw the bra and panty set I found while out shopping today.

"No. Fucking. Way. My beautiful, butterfly."

"Why thank you. I found these today while out shopping and knew that I needed to wear them for you."

"You're an absolutely stunning woman, Ryann," he growled, right before our mouths roughly crashed together. It was the kind of kiss that you felt in every inch of your body. Our tongues greedily invaded each other's mouth. Lacing my fingers behind his neck, Nathan's fists took a tight grip in my hair, continuing to push our mouths together. He stood up from the chair and lifted me so my legs wrapped around his waist, never breaking our kiss, and carried me into our bedroom.

Expecting Nathan to put me down on the bed, I was surprised when I found myself standing in front of our fully open floor to ceiling window. Not as nice as Vegas, but the view from our top floor room wasn't too shabby. "Nice view," I commented.

"The view is perfect from where I'm standing," he whispered in my ear as he pressed his body up against mine. Almost immediately, his hands started exploring my body. He slowly began trailing his fingers along my stomach, goosebumps instantly appearing on my skin. He continued to move up my body until both of his strong hands cupped my breasts. When I felt the slight pain of his thumb and finger pinching my nipple, I couldn't help but moan. The more I moaned, the harder Nathan worked my nipples. It was fucking sensational. When he took one hand off my breast I was tempted to whine, until he dove into my panties. With one hand Nathan continued to pinch both my nipples and with the other he began to gently rub my clit. I honestly don't remember the last time anything had felt that damn good. Leaning forward, I braced myself on the windows to keep from falling, while Nathan used this opportunity to place kisses up and down my back.

"I have been waiting for this night, Ryann. A night that I didn't have to share you with work or old memories. Just us making new memories," he shared as he pulled me back into his arms. "But most of all, butterfly, I've been dying to taste this delicious body of yours."

Nathan picked me up in his arms and gently laid me down on the bed behind us. He covered my body with his, propping himself up on his elbows. "You really are fucking beautiful," he murmured across my lips, then started kissing me.

"You're not too bad yourself, handsome," I quietly replied as I ran my nails up and down his sides. Nathan moved his kisses down my neck and across my chest. I felt my breath hitch the first time his mouth met my breasts. He continued to caress, lick, and gently bite each of my nipples, I could feel my panties starting to get wet. He reached down and dipped his finger deep within my folds, there was no way for me not to scream out his name.

"Mmmm, baby you're so wet. I have been dreaming about what you taste like since the moment I first saw you in that black see through dress you were wearing. Can I taste you, Ryann?" Nathan almost begged.

"Please Nathan. Please."

He moved down my body and pulled my panties off, throwing them to the side. Gently, he moved his hands down and pushed my legs apart, rubbing his fingers in my eager, wet pussy. The moans continued to escape my throat. I couldn't help it. It'd been so long since I'd been touched by a man, I knew I wouldn't be able to hold my orgasm back for much longer.

As soon as Nathan's tongue brushed over my clit I felt like I was going to explode. My hands couldn't help but go straight to his head and to run my fingers through his hair. "Baby, I'm going to cum," I barely got out between breaths.

"You are so sweet, butterfly. So god damn delicious. Cum. Cum on my tongue, Ryann," Nathan said, continuing the assault on my pussy. I couldn't hold back any longer and exploded.

Not even realizing Nathan still had his pants on, he stood up, unbuttoned his jeans and let them fall to the ground. I couldn't help but stare at him the entire time with this stupid shit-eating grin on my face. The man standing in front of me was fucking hot as hell, with perfect muscles, amazing tattoos, and these golden hazel eyes that would melt my panties any day. My mouth immediately started watering the second he pulled down his boxer briefs and let his cock spring free. I didn't have much to compare it to figuring I was with the same man for the last nine years, but Nathan was huge. Having this man inside me was something I was looking forward to.

Nathan walked over to the nightstand and picked up his phone. At first I couldn't help but think what the hell is going on? Please don't let asshole Nathan appear again. Oh, God, please don't take any pictures. Then *Earned It* by The Weekend started playing and I was pissed at myself for thinking the worst again. I heard the unmistakable rip of the condom wrapper. I don't even remember the last time I had sex with a condom. I thought about telling Nathan about not being able to have kids thing, but I didn't think now was the right time.

"Ryann? What's going on in that beautiful mind? Stop thinking and just enjoy," Nathan reminded me. Hovering his body over mine, he barely placed the tip of his cock in my folds, driving me fucking crazy. It was driving me fucking crazy. "Butterfly, are you ok?" he asked as he tucked my hair behind my ears.

I nodded. "I'm more than fine." I bucked my hips up to push him inside me just a little further.

He complied, and continued to slowly move in and out of me as my insides managed to clamp around every inch of him. The way he kissed me each time we moved together sent shockwaves through my core. "You feel so fucking good. So tight around my cock. Baby, I'm not going to last very long."

Knowing that I wasn't far from having a second orgasm myself, I moved my hips to match the rhythm of his. "Go, Nathan," I screamed, while digging my nails into his sides as he pounded the life out of me, which ended with us orgasming together.

Nathan quickly got up and threw the condom away, grabbing us a towel to clean up with. As I laid there thinking about what just happened, I couldn't help but giggle. "What's so funny?" he asked as he started to clean me up.

"Nothing, really. Just Ashlynn was right," I giggled.

"What the hell does that mean?" Nathan asked looking confused and a little upset. "I've never fucked with any of those girls."

"Good. No, she said sleeping with a client could get messy, and she may be right. But is it better to say I slept with my boss?" I asked seriously with a bit a sarcasm. I'm not sure which one came out more.

Nathan laid back down next to me and lifted my chin so that our eyes could meet. "How about saying you made love to your man?"

"I like that."

I spent the next day lounging by the pool and sipping margaritas, thinking about Nathan and what I had planned on doing to him later. But, I also started to think about what it meant to have him as my man when I went back to work the following week? That evening, Nathan insisted that we stay in again. He said he would be willing to share me when we went back to Vegas, but not tonight. We ordered room service, made love almost everywhere in that room, and fell asleep wrapped in each other's arms.

Since Nathan had made it to the final table, I decided to watch the end of the tournament. The whole thing was very intense and quiet. I was so used to a room of rambunctious five-year-olds that this seemed deathly still. I kept trying not to look at Nathan because I didn't want to distract him, but damn he was hard not to look at. After eight long hours, I was thrilled to be able to watch my man take first place. Holy shit, that's a $75,000 paycheck. I barely make that in two years.

After his win, Nathan came over to me and kissed me deeply. "You, butterfly, are my good luck charm."

On the way back to Las Vegas, Nathan noticed my lack of conversation. "What's up?" Nathan asked as he reached over and grabbed my hand.

"How will this all work, Nathan? Us? Me stripping? It all just seems weird," I knew I was rambling but I'd never been in a situation like that before.

"Of all people, Ryann, I understand stripping is a job that you can make great, fast money. Do I like the idea of other men staring at my woman? No. But I do get it. We'll figure us out along the way. I trust you and your limits. But I will ask you not to do any more private rooms with G please." The way he stared at me with those pleading eyes told me I would not turn down his request.

"I can do that, Nathan," I softly said, leaning into his shoulder.

"Keep what's under here for me," he growled as he ran his hand underneath my skirt.

Dark Necessities

The past weekend was one the best damn weekends I have had in a long time. I had a connection with Ryann, a feeling that has not been there in some time. This woman was something special to me, a girl I wanted to get to know better, despite the fact that she was a dancer. I remembered she said that she is only working at *The Cave* while her show was on hiatus for the summer, but I haven't quite figured out why she hasn't talked about her regular show yet. There was some weird shit in Vegas, but she doesn't seem the type to be involved in that. At least, I hope she wasn't

On the way back from Laughlin, Ryann and I decided it might be best if I wasn't at the club so much this week. She told me she only had a few weeks left and needed to make some money before the summer was over and that me being there would be a distraction for her. I had to laugh when she added that she didn't want to see Ashlynn's hands massaging my body. I probably would have argued with her a little more if I hadn't seen on the internet that G had to go back to Boston for a family emergency. I will just let Ryann think she won this one.

After spending the last three nights wrapped in my woman's arms, the last thing I wanted to do was let my butterfly go. I called Molly and she had no problem staying one more night. For the money I was paying her, there shouldn't be any problems. I wanted one more night where I knew Ryann's tits would only be seen by me.

Before going to bed, Ryann wanted to take a shower after the drive home. We walked directly to her bedroom, put our stuff down, and went to the shower. I turned on the water for her and went to leave respecting her privacy.

"Hey, where are you going?" she asked when she grabbed my hand.

"Giving you some privacy, baby," I responded.

"Nope, not this time," she smiled at me. "This time I need help washing those hard to reach places."

Before the words even finished leaving her mouth, both of us were ripping off each other's clothes. The slightest touch of her nails sent an immediate spark to my dick. Fuck, I needed to be inside her again. Once we stepped into the shower, Ryann instantly relaxed into my body, and allowed the hot water to wash over us. She had to be feeling my erection pushing into her back, there was no way of denying what this girl does to me.

Twisting her around, I was able to kiss her beautiful lips. *God, I already am addicted to kissing these lips.* "I need to hurry up and get you clean," I growled as I tilted her head back under the water and kissed all the way down her neck.

"Mmmm," she moaned, "what's your hurry?" She began to run her wet, soapy hand up and down my already extremely hard dick.

"Because I need to fuck you, baby," I practically growled on her tits.

Ryann placed her fingers under my chin and pulled my eyes down to meet hers. "Be honest with me, Nathan. Are you clean?" I nodded yes. I didn't even remember the last time I had sex with anyone. "So am I," she said.

"Are you on the pill?" I asked.

Looking down, I could tell she didn't want to answer. *Holy fuck.* No way would Ryann be one of those women trying to trap me in a pregnancy for my money. And if she was she couldn't be that stupid to tell me before we had sex.

"No, I'm not on the pill," she admitted. It was hard to tell with all the water, but it appeared as if she was crying. "I can't have kids, Nathan. That's why Lucas left me. He didn't just leave me out of the blue. He left me because I am broken."

"You're fucking kidding me right?" I almost screamed at her.

Ryann shook her head. "No, and I understand if you want to leave."

I lifted my girl up by her perfectly rounded ass and she wrapped her legs around my waist. "Look at me," I demanded. "Why the hell would I want to leave you, Ryann?"

"Because I can never give you what you want. So why would you want to start anything with me? Because I'm...broken," she whispered so softly I could barely hear her.

"My butterfly tattoos are for my two babies that I lost."

"Oh, Ryann, you are not broken. What we have going here isn't about whether or not you can have kids. This is about us. You and I enjoying the fuck out of each other. And right now...I am going to enjoy fucking you again."

Gripping her fingers around my neck, Ryann pulled herself just slightly up, and carefully slipped my cock inside her pussy.

"Holy shit, butterfly. You are so wet. You have no idea how damn good it feels to be inside you."

"I think I do," she said as she kissed my lips. She began to bounce faster on my dick.

Feeling her slickness coat my dick was almost too much for me to bear. Each time I was with Ryann, it was better than the time before. But this time, feeling her, with nothing separating us was fucking great. I was ready to cum again almost as soon as she put my dick in. But do I cum in her or do I pull out? Not that I didn't trust Ryann, but I was worth a lot of money so I take my precautions seriously. Fuck it, even if Ryann hadn't explained to me that she couldn't get pregnant the only place I would want to be cumming is inside my girl's pussy.

We both laid there that night obviously restless in our thoughts. I was planning on telling her about Ella before she arrived the following week, but really what was I supposed to say now? Sorry you can't have kids, but hey I have a nine-year-old daughter. Something about that seemed just a bit coldhearted. Instead I pulled Ryann in closer and held her tight

"Butterflies represent pregnancy loss. I have two angel babies and my tattoos are for each one," Ryann quietly confessed into my chest. I pulled her in tighter. "We lost the first baby eight weeks into the pregnancy. That's why this one is pink and blue," she continued and pointed to the top butterfly. "And the day we were to find out the sex of our second baby, we found she had also already gone to heaven. That's the pink one here."

"Thank you for sharing with me. I have a serious question. Now that I know the meanings, is it still ok that I call you butterfly? The last thing I want to do is upset you, beautiful." I asked her.

She leaned up and began to place kisses along my jawline. "I wouldn't have it any other way."

I pulled Ryann on top of me so that we were face to face, bodies pressing tightly against each other. "Ryann, I'm going to do everything I can to make you feel like the most beautiful woman in the world. I hate that asshole forever making you feel like you were broken. I'm going to fuck you again just to show you how not broken you really are."

Lifting her small body up, I lowered her onto my rock hard dick. I fucking loved having Ryann on top. From this angle, it was the most beautiful sight. I could see my dick sliding in and out of her dripping pussy. When she lifted herself up, I would see her juices glisten all over me. Each time she moved, her tits would bounce in my face. I fucking loved her tits. But the best sight of all was her gorgeous face.

My butterfly could not hide the pleasure on her face, showing me she loved this as much as I did.

We collapsed onto each other, both out of breath and exhausted. I knew I should get up and get something to clean us up, but the thought of her with me inside her caused me not to move.

"What are you doing for the 4th of July?" I asked her.

"Working. Rose says its hella busy," Ryann laughed knowing all too well that I hated that word. It irritated me.

"Yeah. The Red, White and Boobs party. It's a fun time. But before that? Do you want to go to a barbeque at my sister's place with me?"

"Oh…meeting the family already, huh?" she cooed.

"Yes, but just my sister and her son. Her husband is currently overseas, and my parents live in Los Angeles," I explained.

"Sounds like fun," she answered. We continued to kiss until we fell asleep.

I decided not to go to the club for the next couple nights. I knew Ryann needed the job, and I didn't want to do anything that would make her feel uncomfortable. What I really wanted to do was tell her I made plenty of money to take care of her, and she could come over each night so she could be my own personal stripper. But that made me uncomfortable just thinking about it. I couldn't even imagine saying that to her.

I used the free time to get Ella's room ready and set

myself to a normal sleeping schedule. Playing poker and owning a strip club were two occupations that definitely keep you up all night. Then again so will a nine-year-old little girl. This year before she came I decided to give her entire room a makeover. Jordyn told me how well Ella did in school and how much she was growing up, so I thought I would do something special for her. I converted her room from little girl princesses to what was more for my young lady. No matter what, she would always be my baby girl.

I also couldn't stop myself from thinking about the discussion Ryann and I had the other night. The fact that jerk of an ex-husband left her because she couldn't have kids was horrible. I would always look at my wife as a blessing, and if we were lucky enough to have kids that would be a bonus. A marriage should be about choosing to be with a person because you loved them not because of what they could give to you.

By Friday night, I didn't want to stay away from *The Cave*, my friends, or Ryann anymore. Plus, I heard that G was back in town. I trusted Ryann, but I didn't trust him as far as I could throw him. I decided to sit at the main bar rather than hide up in my booth, especially when I saw that Jeremy, Rose's husband, was there.

"Hey, buddy. Haven't seen you around in a while," I said, grabbing a bar stool next to him.

"Yeah, strip clubs are usually not my thing. But Rose and I are going out tonight so I decided to come down here and hang until she gets off," Jeremy told me.

"Hey nuts, missed ya," Ryann said in her sultry Vaughn voice. People knew we were hanging out together, but we figured it was best not to tell people at the club about us being a couple. If that's what we were. Wrapping my arm around her waist, I pulled her in close to me. I wanted so damn bad to be possessive of my girl. I saw Jeremy look Ryann up and down. Since they've been best friends since they were seventeen, and Ryann being his best friend's wife, it must be weird for him to have seen her tits. Tonight, Ryann wore a pink G-string, a see through net skirt, and a matching pink net top. Only problem was Ryann had nothing on under that top. Her nipples were perfectly poking through the net.

"Hey, *Vaughn*," Jeremy smirked. "Come give me a hug. I haven't seen you in while." Jeremy pulled Ryann in tight, almost too tight. I glanced over at Rose to see if she noticed but she was busy helping customers. Maybe Ryann hadn't told Rose about us yet. Jeremy just seemed to hug her a little too tight for my liking.

After they separated, I bluntly put my arm around Ryann's waist and pulled her back into me. "You booked for the next hour?" I asked her.

"Nope. Just working the floor. No VIP rooms for me. Bosses orders," she made sure to look at me and wink.

"Now you are," I grabbed her by the arm, pulled her across the dance floor, and into one of the private rooms.

"C'mon, Nathan. We really are busy and I need the money before summer break is over." She tried to escape but I blocked the door.

"Butterfly, tonight I'm a paying customer. I miss you. And I hate to say it but, I miss strippers too. So I figured I could spend an hour with my favorite girl and get both fixes taken care of." I sat down on the bench seat and pulled her down on top of my lap.

"Wow, you could get your fix of me in only an hour, huh?" she teased.

"Baby, I don't think I could ever get my fix of you," I told her as I went to lean in for a kiss. She put her fingers up to stop me and started to back away.

"Nope. For the next hour you're a client. You don't get these lips until we get home tonight. Unless that's how you want me to treat all my clients."

I tried to persuade her to spend the rest of the evening with me, but she kept insisting that she didn't want to take money from me and this was her job. Since we were sleeping together, I saw her point that taking money from me made her feel like a hooker, but isn't that what couple's do? Share money. She still didn't see my point. We made our way back to the bar, where I watched as Vaughn started making her way around the room. Honestly, thinking of her as Vaughn while we were at the club was the only way I could keep myself sane. Here she was Vaughn, and at home she was my Ryann. I will admit, I loved to watch my girl dance. The way she moved her hips was so fucking sexy. But it's different from when I used to watch Jordyn dance. With her, it turned me on to watch her dance for other men. With Ryann, it makes me jealous as fuck. Watching her on stage is a whole other story. The stage dance she does with Vanessa sends a raging hard on to my dick every time I see it.

As the night started to wind down, all I wanted to do was get Ryann home to "Netflix and Chill", have her lay her head in my lap as I run my fingers through her thick hair. By the exhausted look on her face, I think she was going to be more into watching Netflix than the chilling I wanted to do.

"I'll ask Vanessa for a ride home tonight since you rode the Harley here," Ryann told me.

"Don't. Meet me out back as soon as you've changed," I demanded.

What Ryann didn't know was that I bought her a helmet of her own this week. I needed her on the back of my bike with me, to feel her arms tightly holding around my waist as we rode through the streets of Las Vegas. Nothing sexier than a hot woman on a beautiful bike.

A few minutes later Ryann walked out the back door. "What's going on Nathan? I assumed you'd bring the truck tonight since we decided to stay at my place."

I handed her the box and could see the surprised look on her face. "What's this?" she asked.

"Well, usually when someone hands you a box to open, it's a gift," I said sarcastically.

"Nathan, really?" she said almost sounding disappointed.

"Just open it. It's honestly more for me than you anyways." That caused her to lift her eyebrows at me.

She opened the box and found the sleek red helmet just for her. I saw the instant smile appear on her face. "Really? For me?" she asked.

"Nope. It's for Damon. I just thought I'd show you first," I joked. I took the box from her hands and placed it on the ground, pulling her in close to me. "Of course it's for you, butterfly. I want any excuse to have your body pressed up against mine. You are sexy as hell. This bike is also quite sexy." She laughed. Not being able to control myself, I lowered my lips onto hers and kissed her sexy mouth. "And together the two of you are going to make me fucking crazy."

"Sounds hot," she whispered back, leaning down and grabbing her helmet. She walked over to my bike, threw one leg over and climbed to the back. That right there was the best fucking thing I saw all night. Instant hard-on. "Well are you going to take me for a ride?" she asked.

"Do you want to go straight home?" I had an idea up my sleeve if she wasn't too tired.

"Not anymore," she replied.

I climbed on my bike, started the engine, and felt Ryann's arms cling around my waist. I seriously wanted to fuck her right then and there. But I decided it probably wasn't the best thing to do in the parking lot of a strip club. Instead we made a quick stop at a local coffee shop, filled up my thermos, got some muffins and took off. We rode for about thirty minutes until we hit my quiet spot out in the desert.

"Okay… Middle of the desert wasn't really what I was expecting this morning," Ryann said as she pulled off her helmet.

"Last time I tried to take you somewhere it backfired on me, remember?" Grabbing the thermos and the food, I motioned her to follow me. We climbed up the back of a large rock and made ourselves comfortable. "I found this spot a few years back on a ride. I just needed to get away. It was about sunrise when I stopped to have a smoke. I climbed up here and watched the sun rising and thought it was the most beautiful thing I had ever seen."

"Smoke?" she asked quizzically.

"Yes, *mom*," I once again replied in my smart ass tone. "Once in a while I smoke a joint to relax. Like now." I pulled out the joint I had thrown in the muffin bag without Ryann looking. She scrunched up her face and gave me the cutest disapproving look. "I will take that as you don't smoke," I laughed.

"I did a little in college, but not since. Wasn't really my thing. But I'm not necessarily against it," she defended herself.

"I'm going to take a few hits. Would you like some?" I wasn't a pusher but I'd definitely offer. I could see the look of contemplation in her eyes.

"Why not," she said with a shrug. "Reckless abandon has been my motto this summer." We took a few hits, drank our coffee and ate breakfast almost silently as we watched the sun come up. Well, Ryann watched the sun come up. I couldn't seem to take my eyes off her. I wanted to ask her about her show and what her plans were after the summer hiatus but I figured she would tell me when she was ready. I thought this might be a good time to tell her about Ella.

She interrupted my thoughts with her question, "Have you ever brought any other girls to this spot with you?"

"Just one," I answered.

"Jordyn?"

"Hell no. I didn't find this spot until long after her. No. Ella Marie is the only other girl I have brought here."

"Are you ready to tell me about the tattoo?" she asked.

I nodded. "Ryann," I took a deep breath. "Ella is my daughter." I watched the surprise play across her face. "She was the only good thing that happened from Jordyn and me. She's nine. She's beautiful. And she will be here next week."

"Well, okay then."

"Please tell me you are okay with this," I pleaded.

She cupped my face in her hands. "Nathan, I will admit it's a bit of surprise at six a.m. when I'm slightly stoned to find out you have a daughter. But I'll be fine. We will be fine." I hated that word fine.

"Let's go to my place and get some sleep for a few hours before I meet your family," she suggested, standing up and leading us back to my bike.

As soon as we got back to Ryann's place, she crawled in bed and fell right asleep. I could see the exhaustion in her face, and now I've just hit her with another ton of bricks. Maybe I should have waited to tell her about Ella until after she met my sister since I knew how nervous she was about that. But something told me I needed to tell her this morning, and I wasn't going to lie when she asked me if I had brought any other girls to my sunrise rock. Ella is my world and always will be. I wanted Ryann to be a part of my world but it had to include Ella.

The shower was already going, when I woke up late that morning. Ryann was in there quietly singing some country song on the radio I didn't recognize. God even her voice was like heaven.

"Good morning, butterfly," I said as I snuck in her bathroom.

"Hi, handsome. You going to join me?" she seductively asked.

"Well, only because you asked so nicely," I quipped back.

Ryann wrapped her arms around my waist and began kissing my chest. "I'm sorry for getting all funky this morning."

"Why are you sorry? You have nothing to be sorry for. Me telling you I have a daughter was something huge."

"I just didn't expect you to say you had a kid since you've never mentioned her before. But seriously I'm fine. Plus, I was a little stoned," Ryann laughed.

"With you and me, beautiful, there is still a lot to learn."

"I know something I still want to learn," she

whispered.

"Oh yeah? What's that?" I asked. Hoping my assumptions were correct.

"How you taste," she said looking directly in my eyes.

Dropping to her knees, she took my cock in her beautiful mouth and ran her lips up and down my length, using her tongue to swirl my tip. It felt fucking fabulous. Every once in a while, she would look up and our eyes would meet. The connection between us was intense. I had no desire to look away while my woman was anywhere near my dick. I reached down to play with her bouncing tits. Everything about Ryann drove me over the edge.

"Baby are you sure you want to taste me?"

"I can't fucking wait," she mumbled against my cock.

Moving my hands from her tits to her hair, I gripped fists full of her and started to move faster, fucking her mouth. Fuck, she felt so good wrapped around my cock. With one long push, I exploded in Ryann's mouth. The look of her licking her lips when she was done, made me hard again almost instantly. My dick just couldn't get enough of this woman.

"Turn around," I ordered. She did as I told her to. Bending her over, I grabbed another fist full of her hair and gently placed my cock right on the edge of her clit, moving back and forth. I wanted to make sure Ryann was ready when I took her again.

"Fuck me, Nathan," she begged. Hearing her say my

name was I all I needed. I put my hardening cock inside her wet pussy and continued to fuck her until we both exploded.

**

We were driving to my sister's house for the barbeque, when Ryann asked, "So who was the last girl you brought over to meet your sister?"

"Umm...honestly. Jordyn."

"You're kidding me right? No pressure or anything," she let out a nervous laugh.

Ryann was quiet most of the drive to my sister's. I guess it was to be expected with the events of the last twenty-four hours. Her nerves seemed to get worse the closer we got. I could see it on her face. We hadn't discussed how I would introduce her since we hadn't really discussed her being my girlfriend. But in my mind that's what she was. I haven't told my sister much about her, except that we met at the club, and that she's fucking beautiful.

When we pulled up I could see Ryann shaking. Placing my hand on her shoulder, I sought to reassure her. "It's okay, butterfly. They don't bite."

"How old is your nephew?" I thought it was an odd question, but I answered anyway.

"He just had his sixth birthday. Why?"

Before she could answer, my nephew, Jackson came running out the door, and tried to jump on my back. "Uncle Nate! Uncle Nate! You made it!" he yelled jumping up and down.

"Of course I would buddy. You know I wouldn't miss swimming with you," I said as I spun around and picked him up.

"There's a surprise for you in the house too," Jackson whispered.

"I don't think you are supposed to share surprises, buddy," I told him. "Hey, I want you to meet my girlfriend..."

Jackson jumped out of my arms so quick I practically dropped him. "Ms. McKennan! Mom, look! Uncle Nate's girlfriend is Ms. McKennan." My nephew ran into Ryann's arms giving her one of the biggest hugs I'd ever seen him give anyone.

"What. The. Fuck," I whispered under my breath. I remembered the night that I first saw Ryann, I recognized her from somewhere. Seeing her hanging out with all the girls from *The Cave*, I just assumed I'd seen Ryann around the club. But holy fuck, I remember now, Ryann McKennan was Jackson's kindergarten teacher last year.

Then out of nowhere, Ella came up and put her little arms around my waist. "Well, I was supposed to be your surprise, Daddy, but Jackson knowing your girlfriend looks like a bigger surprise."

Angels Fall

As Nathan pulled off the freeway, my mind started reeling. What were the chances that his sister would live in the same neighborhood where I taught? There were not very many schools in this area of North Las Vegas, so if his nephew was elementary school age he would attend the school I worked at. Maybe I'd get lucky and his nephew would be in middle school or better yet, not even in school yet. I couldn't believe we'd never talked about it. When we pulled up to the house, my body started shaking uncontrollably. Something in my gut told me this was going to be bad.

Opening the door to exit Nathan's truck, my entire body froze when I saw a little blonde haired boy poking his head out of the door. *NO! NO! NO!* I screamed in my head. Nathan's nephew, Jackson, was in my kindergarten class last year. And to make matters worse his sister, Cristina, volunteered in my class and worked closely with the PTA. My whole fucking world was about to blow up.

Jumping into my arms, Jackson gave me one of those hugs only he could do. Throughout this past school year, I'd grown close to him. I knew his father was deployed overseas which caused me to give him that little bit of extra attention.

He often talked about his Uncle Nate coming over to play and swim with him, but never in in million years would I have thought that my Nathan would be my student's Uncle Nate from class.

I felt the bile rise up in my throat as this adorable little boy gripped tighter around my neck. I was about to throw up. "Jackson, honey could you show me to the restroom?" I asked him.

"Of course, Ms. McKennan. Oh my goodness. I'm so happy my favorite teacher is here to go swimming with me," he bounced with joy.

Jackson took my hand and led me into the house. For completely different reasons, I couldn't bring myself to look at either Nathan or Cristina. I dug through my purse and found my phone and sent Rose a text.

Me: I have never needed my best friend more. Come get me NOW! No joke.

Rose: Are you ok? Are you hurt? Where are you?

Me: No I am not ok. No I am not hurt. Things are bad. Pick me up on the corner by Rock Canyon Elementary.

Rose: WTF? Where's Nathan?

Me: Just come get me please.

Rose: Give me 20 minutes. I'm on my way.

I walked out of the bathroom to see Nathan waiting for me in the hallway. "Care to explain, Ms. McKennan?" he asks.

"Please, Nathan. Not here. Not now. Rose is coming to get me so you can spend time with your family. I need to go now," I cried.

"Let me take you home, Ryann."

"No. I can't be around you. Or anyone for that matter. She's meeting me at the school on the corner," I told him.

"Ryann," he softly said my name.

"Ms. McKennan," Jackson came running in the hallway where Nathan and I were talking. "Are you ready to go swimming now?"

"No, sweetie. I'm sorry, I'm not feeling very well. My friend is coming to get me so I can go lie down for a while," I kneeled down and explained to him.

"Okay. I understand," Jackson said sadly. "Uncle Nate, are you leaving too?"

"For a few minutes, buddy. But I'll be right back after Ms. McKennan's friend picks her up."

Nathan guided me out the front door with his hand on the small of my back. I couldn't bring myself to make eye contact with Cristina. I had no idea what Nathan had told her about me. And yet at the same time I hadn't told Nathan the truth.

As soon as I was out of sight of Nathan's family, the tears started running down my face. I didn't want to have the conversation with Nathan about me being a broke ass teacher in the middle of the street in the neighborhood I taught in. I needed to get the fuck out of there.

"Ryann, stop, please, baby," Nathan said placing his hands on my shoulders. "Talk to me, butterfly."

"What, Nathan!" I yelled. "What the hell do you want me to say right now? My show that is on hiatus for the summer is right there. Rock Canyon Elementary School. I teach kindergarten. Last year, my divorce, left my life pretty well fucked up. At the beginning of the summer I made the choice to move home with my mother and her nudist boyfriend because I was that damn broke. But then my wonderful best friend convinced me to strip and now my entire life is fucked up and going straight down the drain."

"I don't understand, Ryann. Is this because of Cristina and Jackson?" Nathan asked. I could see the utter confusion on his face.

"Nathan, where did you tell Cristina we met?" I asked, my frustration obviously growing.

"Fuck. At the club," he answered.

Before anything else could be said, Rose's truck pulled up, but it wasn't Rose driving. Jeremy had come to get me. He rolled down the window. "Get in, Ryann."

"Jeremy, I would never hurt her," Nathan assured him.

"Dude, that's between you two. But when Rose gets that upset it's best not to let her drive, man," Jeremy answered. I closed the truck door and we drove off. My phone chimed a few minutes later.

Nathan: I will see you tonight at the party butterfly.

Seriously? Did he really think I was still going to the Red, White, and Boobs party? I didn't know what to do anymore. My life had seriously just blown up before my eyes. I was sure that Cristina had already texted the entire mom tree to let them know the new teacher moonlights as a stripper. I guess, I would no longer be moonlighting and this might become my full-time job. Where the hell did my life go some damn wrong?

I could see Rose pacing in the driveway as soon as Jeremy and I pulled up. "I'm sorry to ruin your plans today," I apologized to her as I jumped out of the truck.

Making our way up the stairs, Rose said, "Honey, you didn't ruin anything. C'mon to my room. Let's talk. Looks like you need me."

"So I'm busted," I told her.

"What the hell does that even mean?" Rose asked.

I explained to her that I met Nathan's sister and nephew and that they just happened to know me as Ms. McKennan, kindergarten teacher extraordinaire, and that Nathan had already told his sister we met at the club. I also mentioned that Cristina is sweet as hell but has been known to be the PTA gossip mom.

"So pretty much my career is over when this gets out. And secrets always have a way of getting out," I reminded her.

"Maybe Nathan could ask her not to say anything?" Rose said trying to sympathize with my situation.

"Really? Gossip always happens. Trust me. And the moms around school are hella bad gossipers. You should know that."

"So, now what?" Rose asked.

"I have no idea. Nathan sent me a text as soon as I left telling me he'd see me tonight at the party, but I'm going to skip it."

"Ryann, tonight would be big money for you."

"Yeah, I know but I think I may disappear for a few days. Can you take me home please?"

Without any argument, Rose took me home. I told her I wouldn't be answering any calls or texts, but she had my permission to track my phone to make sure I was okay. Rose was always the mom in our group of friends. She offered to explain to Damon why I wasn't there so that I didn't have to. She was definitely that one person who was always looking out for me.

Not long after I got home, Roxy and I got in my Challenger and just drove. I headed east and figured I would find someplace along the river for my dog and I to crash for the next couple days. I had no idea what was going to happen next in my life. Was I going to lose my job? Would I have to become a full-time stripper? What was going to happen between Nathan and me? Fuck, it honestly was all just too much to handle.

I wasn't normally a heavy drinker, but when shit gets too messed up I have a tendency to down a few bottles of wine. Slightly drunk and definitely lonely, I grabbed my phone and started to scroll through my social media sites. Seeing nothing exciting in Facebook land, I decided to check the Vaughn Haley Instagram for anything new. Not that I expected there to be. Oh, one new follower and a couple of direct messages. *Curious.* Who the hell is RG87NEP? Oh holy hell, it was G.

RG87NEP- Hi baby girl. Sorry I had to leave. Family thing.

RG87NEP- Don't think I have forgotten about that dinner invitation. I still have every intention of taking you out.

Shit, I didn't know how this whole Instagram thing worked. Did he know that I'd seen the messages? Did that mean I was obligated to respond? Did I want to respond? What about Nathan? My best answer to everything was to finish the bottle of wine and pass out until the next day. And then call Rose.

The next morning, I woke up with a headache the size of Montana. Now I remembered why I don't drink wine. As much as I wanted to run, being by myself was not the best of ideas. I needed to go home and figure this mess out. I sent Rose a quick text telling her to meet me at the pool in a couple of hours. I took a few aspirin, grabbed a quick shower, and hoped like hell that yesterday was just a bad dream. Even though I knew it wasn't.

A few hours later, Rose and I were basking in the mid-day heat of the Las Vegas summer. "Has Nathan tried to contact you since you left yesterday?" Rose asked.

"Yeah, a couple texts and voicemails telling me he's worried about me and to please call him," I told her.

"And have you?"

"No, Rose, I haven't." My real bitch attitude was coming out. "What am I supposed to say? Sorry I didn't trust you enough to tell you about my real job? It doesn't matter either way because we're done. I do need to call and tell him that."

"Excuse me, but why?" Rose was practically yelling at me.

"Really? I can't show my face around his sister or his family. I was fricken mortified. Nice to meet you, Mr. and Mrs. Sims. Why yes, I was Jackson's kindergarten teacher and now I'm Nathan's stripper girlfriend. C'mon! Give me a break, Rose! And plus dating my boss was never a good idea in the first place," I explained, getting upset.

"Boss? What in the hell are talking about? Are you still on a wine drunk?"

"Shit. Yeah. Well, Nathan is a silent partner in *The Cave*. Oh! And to make matters worse, G has sent me a couple messages on Instagram thanks to that lovely Vaughn Haley account."

"Wow, girl, things really are fucked up for you at the moment," she laughed sarcastically.

"Gee thanks."

"Stop. You're being typical, Ryann. Stop overthinking things that haven't even happened yet. You've already played out the worst case scenario in your head and decided that your life is over. Talk to Nathan, and figure out what you two really are and what you want. Talk to him about what's going on with Cristina, and see if there's anything you can do to keep her mouth shut. And as far as G goes, I don't know what to tell you. He doesn't have the best rep, but his tips could set you up for the rest of the year."

"Well, that helped none." I laughed.

"I do have one really important question for you. Is Nathan as good in bed as he looks?" Rose cocked her head to the side waiting for me to actually answer her. *What the hell?*

**

On Tuesday morning, I mustered up the courage to at least send Nathan a text. I figured I'd be safe since I knew he had a tournament at the Bellagio for the next couple of days and shouldn't be coming to the club. At least I hoped he wouldn't with Ella being in town. She seemed like such a sweet young girl. It sucked that I wouldn't actually get to meet her. Especially since I was genuinely starting to have real feelings for Nathan. It all just felt so fucked up.

Was Rose right? Was I just being typical Ryann? Overthinking, speculating the worst case scenario, running for cover when the bombs hadn't even been launched yet. I mean I had no idea if Cristina would say anything to the school or to the other mothers, but I was acting as if she'd already ratted me out. Maybe Nathan and I could get past all this. But the real question was, could I? With that lurking question, I sent Nathan a text.

Me: Nathan - I have enjoyed the time we have spent together but I can't do this anymore. I'm sorry.

It only took him two minutes to respond.

Nathan- Really? A text Ryann? This discussion isn't over butterfly.

When Nathan showed his assertive side, I became completely aroused. The way he was able to take control of a situation, take control of me. All of me; body, mind and heart started a slow fire within me that I yearned to have stroked to flame. Yes, as much as I couldn't admit it to myself, Nathan had stolen my heart. I knew long ago that he possessed my body but I struggled with wanting to give him my heart. The night we laid together and talked about my tattoos, my angels, that was the turning point for me. And now I was breaking both our hearts.

    **

I needed to get back to *The Cave* and get my mind off of my real life troubles. It was one of those nights where I just needed to have a few drinks, dance with my friends and make some fucking money. The drama-llama was not welcome. Vanessa and I would be doing our *Hot for Teacher* routine, which continued to bring in buckets of cash for us, and we had a crazy group performance to the new Meghan Trainor song. I needed to just forget my life for as long as I could.

I had on my naughty school girl outfit but opted to go with my fiery red wig and green contacts. That combination gave me an Irish look that guys seemed to go nuts for. The club was packed for a Tuesday. As we got into the summer months it was all about the weddings in Las Vegas, which meant bachelor parties, and more money in my G-string.

As I sat at the bar having a drink, I stole glances up at Nathan's booth to see if he had snuck in without me noticing. Part of me really wanted to see him even though I knew it would not be a good thing. The other part of me wanted to run. Run and never look back. My mother used to tease me, saying I had "lots of parts."

"Did you ever talk to him?" Rose came up from behind me and asked.

"I sent him a text," I sadly answered.

"Really? As close as you two were becoming and you took the chicken shit way out? That's kind of low," she scolded before she walked away from me.

Wow. My best friend of the last twenty years was giving me shit about this? I should be pissed off at her. If it wasn't for Rose and her wonderful suggestion of me working here at *The Cave* I wouldn't be in this predicament. I'd be back in California looking for teaching jobs, not wondering if I would still have one in a month. But as much as I wanted to, I couldn't blame Rose for all the mess I was in. Ultimately the responsibility all fell on me.

"Hey, girl. How are you doing tonight?" Vanessa asked as she joined me.

"I'm fine. Why? What's up?" I asked.

"Well, there's a bachelor party going on in the sports bar tonight. Have you been there yet?" I shook my head. "The best man has requested a private dance for the groom and asked for the saucy redhead student. You up for it?"

"Of course!" I faked my enthusiasm. "That's what I'm here for right?"

"Good. He's waiting for you in private room number six."

I reluctantly made my way to the private rooms. I hadn't been back there since Nathan and I made the agreement that I would stay on the floor or the stage. My heart was telling me I was making a mistake, but I knew that I needed the money. I put on my Vaughn happy face and got ready to shake my tits in some random guy's face.

Walking into the dimly lit room, I prepared myself to dance for the lucky groom. He didn't seem all that excited, like most of the grooms we got back there. The stiffness of his shoulders told me he was reluctant to participate. The shaking of his legs showed me he was completely anxious. Poor guy. Well, I'd do my best to make sure he was smiling from ear to ear and had a raging hard-on by the time he left.

"Hey, sexy," I said in my seductive stripper voice. "You ready to have a good time before you start your life with the old ball and chain?"

"Sure," he replied, never looking up from his lap.

"*Oh*," I cooed, "we have a shy one here. Well I may just

have to wake you up a little, baby."

"Sorry, strip clubs have never been my thing," he said looking up.

Oh. My. God. I would know that voice anywhere. It was the voice of my dreams for so many years until it became the voice of my nightmares. No, this couldn't be happening. Did I turn on the lights and confirm my suspicions or just run? I had to see. I needed to know. Spinning around, I flicked on the lights.

"Lucas?" I shakily asked.

He peered at me confused, but then as if a lightbulb went on he realized who I was. "Holy fuck. Ryann? What the hell are you doing here?"

I could feel the bile rise in my throat. My knees went weak. My head started spinning. "I would ask you the same, Lucas, but obviously I already know the answer to that."

I opened the door and ran out of the private room as fast as my feet would carry me. When I made it out to the main floor, I continued to run to the dressing room without even looking where I was going. As I came around the last corner, I ran into a six foot three brick wall of a man.

"Baby girl, what's wrong? I've been looking all over for you."

"G," I said, "sorry, I didn't mean to run into you." When I looked away I saw Lucas at the bar talking to Rose.

"Vaughn, are you alright?"

"No I'm not. G, can you please get me out of here?" I asked.

"C'mon. Let's go. My car's out back," He took my hand and led me out to the parking lot.

Without any further thought, I got into G's Range Rover and left. He didn't ask me where I wanted to go; he just started driving. Pulling up in front of the Bellagio Hotel, I wanted to say something like: I couldn't go up to his room or to take me home, but instead I found myself mindlessly following him inside.

I left the club so quickly that I didn't change or even grab my purse. I found myself walking through the swanky Bellagio lobby in only my school girl costume. Once again, I was in the lovely position of everyone staring at me. And yet, I didn't know if they were staring at me or at G. I'd nearly forgotten I was walking around with one of the most famous football players in the NFL.

Quickly making our way to his private suite, my brain started going wild in typical Ryann fashion. What was G expecting? What was I expecting? What the hell would Nathan think when he found out?

My thoughts were interrupted by G's question. "Would you like something more comfortable to wear?"

"Oh, yeah. Sure, I guess," I answered barely paying attention.

He came back out with a large t-shirt for me and a pair of his boxers. "Will this work? Anything else I have will be huge on your teeny little body."

"Thanks," I said, embarrassed.

"Vaughn, stop being shy with me. I don't bite…unless you want me to," he laughed. "No, seriously, I could see you needed someone tonight. Let me be that someone. I've been told I'm like a giant teddy bear."

"Thanks, G. I do need someone," I leaned up on my tiptoes, wrapped my arms around his neck, and kissed his cheek.

"Please call me, Rich," he insisted.

"Okay, Rich. My name is actually Ryann," I cautiously told him.

"Yeah, I had a feeling it wasn't Vaughn Haley," he laughed. "Go get changed, I'll order some room service, pour some drinks, and if you feel like it, we can talk."

Walking into the bathroom, I stopped and stared at my own reflection. I had no idea who the woman in the mirror was anymore. Five years ago, I was the happily married wife of Lucas McKennan. A year ago I was a newly divorced teacher, but I felt like I knew who I was. Today, I had no fucking clue who I was anymore. A teacher, a stripper, in a "sorta" relationship, and now in a NFL player's hotel room. What the hell was I doing?

"Baby girl!" I heard G…Rich…shouting from the other room. "What do you drink?"

"Vodka and cranberry please. I'll be right out," I shouted back. Quickly changing, I threw on Rich's shirt, but

175

his boxers fell right off, so what was the point? I took one more look in the mirror, and let out a long sigh. "Ugh, Ryann. What is happening to you, girl?" I wondered to myself.

I walked back out to the sitting area of the room with Rich's shirt barely covering my ass, but I guess it really didn't matter since he'd seen me totally naked before.

"Thanks for getting me out of there tonight. It's been a few really messed up days," I confessed, taking the vodka and cranberry from him.

"Wanna talk about it baby girl?" he asked me.

I just shrugged. Did I want to talk about it? Especially to a hot NFL playboy? Looking over at Rich, I saw a beautiful man, his broad shoulders holding his strong arms open to hold me. The look in his eyes seemed sweet and sincere, like all he really wanted to do was make sure I was okay. I couldn't resist his invite, and crawled up in his lap, put my head on his chest and allowed my whole body to relax into his. Damn, he felt good. We sat silently on the couch sipping our drinks until the knock from room service interrupted us. Rich carefully set me down on the couch and went to take care of the food.

I didn't think I was hungry until the scent of steak and lobster filled the room. Rich spread everything out on the coffee table. "Ready to eat?" he asked.

"Damn, is this the celebrity extra treatment? I need to do this more often," I giggled as I started to bite into the mouthwatering lobster.

"I'd like that," he said almost too quietly for me to hear. I looked up to find him staring right at me.

Crap. I needed to change the subject and fast. "I have to be honest, I had no idea who you were the first time you came into *The Cave* and I went home and Googled you. So tell me, G, why is it always strippers and porn stars?" I asked with a little wiggle of my eyebrow.

The question must have caught him off guard, he practically choked on his beer when I asked. "Well, they're easy," he laughed.

"What the hell, Rich? That's a messed up thing to say. Is...is that what you think of me?" I asked a bit irritated.

"No, that came out completely wrong. What I mean is that girls in those professions usually don't want serious commitments. No drama relationships. At the moment, my career is my number one focus, not women. And no, Ryann, that's not what I think about you," he calmly responded. "My turn now, what's going on with you and Nathan Sims?"

"You know Nathan?" I asked.

"Yeah, I follow professional poker. I love the game. Now stop changing the subject," he scolded me.

"There was something between us but I broke it off," I answered never looking up from my plate. As much as I know it was for the best, it still pains me to actually say it.

"Do you want to tell me why?"

"Nope, it's complicated." Thankfully he didn't ask again.

"So, tell me what had you hightailing it out of the club like a bat out of hell?"

"That I will tell you, but it will require another drink," I said as I held up my glass for a refill.

I told Rich about my divorce and why Lucas left me, and that to make matters worse, I was called in to give him a private dance for his bachelor party. "Okay, that is one of the most fucked up things I've heard in a while. I think that calls for another drink," he says as he picked up my glass for a refill.

Sitting back on the couch, he summoned me back to his lap. I was actually feeling quite tipsy so I had no problem filling his request. I crawled back up and nestled myself into the same spot I was in before. Rich gently started running his large fingers through my hair. I unconsciously let a lusty moan escape my lips.

"Does that feel good, baby girl?" Rich asked as he softly brushed my hair to the side. He placed soft kisses on the back of my neck. I felt myself starting to give in to his touch. His strong embrace made me feel so safe. Leaning my head back, I allowed his mouth to meet mine. His lips were soft and gentle, yet his tongue wasn't fighting to invade my mouth. He continued to place soft kisses on my lips, with an ever so gentle nibble of my bottom lip. I'm not sure if I actually returned his kiss but I definitely did not push him away.

Rich put both our drinks on the table, picked me up and carried me into his room. He laid me down on the bed and crawled in right next to me. Instantly, I felt a huge knot form in my stomach. Too much to drink or not, I knew that I couldn't sleep with Rich. Even if he was sexy as fuck. Nathan's face kept creeping into my mind. I remembered how angry he was when he even thought I slept with G. Broken up or not, I don't want to cause Nathan anymore pain.

"Rich, I can't have sex with you," I meekly said.

"Baby girl, I didn't expect you to. You aren't like most of the girls I've met at clubs. I can sense this higher level of respect for yourself and that you wouldn't sleep with me just because I'm Richard Grovanski," he told me.

"Thank you."

"But that doesn't mean I'm not going to hold you, kiss you, and make you feel safe."

We laid together for the next few hours wrapped in each other's bodies, kissing, laughing, and just having a good time together. Rich was the type of guy that would make sure you were safe and smiling in any situation. We continued to drink and he made me forget the thoughts of my beyond horrible week. Eventually, we fell asleep in each other's arms.

I awoke the next morning with another raging headache. I really needed to stop this drinking thing. I heard Rich singing in the shower, and fuck he sounded sexy. Not only was he an amazing athlete, but a decent singer too. As I laid there listening, the ache between my legs started to grow for him. Thank God the water stopped and Rich got out of the shower before I allowed myself to give in to temptation. I did not need any more confusion in my life.

He walked out of the bathroom with nothing but a towel wrapped around his waist. Every defined chest muscle was glistening with drops of water, his six pack looked good enough to eat off. The man in front in me was absolutely delicious. And yet he wasn't the meal I was craving.

"Good morning, baby girl," he smiled. "How are you feeling this morning?"

I groaned and put the covers back over my head. "Can I just stay in bed all day?"

He leaned in closely, pulled the blankets down and gently brushed his lips against mine. "I would love nothing more than to keep you locked up with me all day but I have a feeling that would get us in some trouble. And the last thing I want is to be another complication for you. But I'm still taking you out," he said matter-of-factly. "Now get up. Go take a shower and breakfast will be here when you get out."

As the hot water ran over my body in one of the most luxurious showers I've ever stepped foot in, I let my mind wander over the events of the last few weeks and where my life was at. I felt like I was in the middle of a giant shit-storm and I kept getting deeper and deeper with each move I made. And now if I was worried about Cristina before, I should sure as hell be worried about Lucas—considering he worked for the same school district I did. I never thought running into Rich would be the best part of my night. It was probably time to come clean with Nathan and everyone else and let the pieces fall where they might.

"Hurry up, baby girl, breakfast is here," Rich shouts

from the other room. I quickly finished up, dried off and threw on a robe that was hanging on the door, since I had nothing else with me except a stripper costume.

"Smells great," I said as I walked out drying my blonde hair.

"Hmm...natural blonde, sexy, baby girl," he pointed out in that sexy Boston accent.

"Yup, natural California blonde. Did you order me clothes?" I asked seeing some clothes hanging on a rack.

"Yeah, I had them send up a few different sizes and styles. Pick something to wear home. You definitely can't wear your school girl costume. Though I wouldn't object," he said coming up behind me and putting his arms around my waist. "Now let's eat, get dressed and get you home. I have a feeling there are a whole lot of people wondering where the fuck you are."

"You know, in all the confusion last night, that wasn't something I even thought about. Crap, I wouldn't be surprised if Rose doesn't have an APB out for me by now."

An hour later, Rich dropped me off at the club. It was after eleven so I knew Damon would be in working on the books, which was to my advantage as I needed to get my purse.

Because it was before hours, I had to be buzzed in through the back door. I waved to Damon as I saw the camera turn toward me. He let me in.

"Good morning, Vaughn. Here to get your car?" Damon

asked coldly.

"Yeah. Horrible experience last night. I'm very sorry if I worried anyone," I tried to explain.

Damon put up his hand to stop me. "We all were very worried about you, Vaughn. But then Nathan came in and told us he saw you at the Bellagio with G, so we knew where you were." I think my jaw just about hit the ground. "And then it was all confirmed this morning when TMZ broke story of Richard Grovanski's new stripper girlfriend." *What. The. Fuck?*

Lovin' Lately

I walked back into my sister's house dumbfounded. I was trying to figure out what exactly just happened. Ryann was Jackson's teacher. *Holy shit!* This was insane. I knew I recognized her but never in a million years did I guess it was from the few times I went to school with my nephew because my brother-in-law was overseas.

"Nathan, what the heck is going on?" Cristina hit me as soon as I walked back in. My good PTA mom of a sister wouldn't dare say a cuss word.

"I honestly have no idea," I responded sitting down and putting my head in my hands. "Apparently, my girlfriend is a kindergarten teacher."

"Yeah, well I got that part. What I don't understand is how you met her at the club?" she asked.

"C'mon, let's grab something to drink and go sit out back and I'll tell you what I know about Ryann McKennan and maybe you can help me feel in some blanks," I told Cristina. We grabbed a couple beers and moved outside so Jackson could enjoy the afternoon swimming.

When I walked into the backyard I saw Ella do a cannonball in the pool off the diving board. In all the chaos, I completely forgot she was here.

"J-Ella Bean! Come here, sweet girl and give your old dad a hug," I shouted as she swam toward me.

"Daddy!" she jumped out and gave me a big, wet hug. "Aunt Cristina helped me get out here early for the big Las Vegas firework show and then a slumber party with Jackson! Can I get back in now?"

"Yeah, go have fun," I told her and kissed her on the top of her head.

I walked over to my sister. "Thank you for bringing her early. Slumber party?" I asked.

"I figured you were going to the party at *The Cave* so I told the kids we would have a slumber party tonight. Okay so now dish, big brother. I need to know the gossip," she said eyes wide.

"Oh, hell no, Cristina. This stays between us. I won't say a word if I can't trust you with this, I won't say anything."

"I'm just kidding," she defended herself.

"No, Cristina. I need to be able to trust you," I demanded seriously. Besides Damon or Vanessa, I really didn't have anyone else I could trust. And I really didn't want to talk to either one of them.

"I'm sorry, Nathan. Of course you can trust me," she put her hand on my shoulder to let me know she was serious. I told her what I knew about Ryann. Obviously, I knew nothing about her teaching so Cristina filled me in on that.

"She's been a kindergarten teacher at Rock Canyon for two years and everyone loves her. Beyond that, I don't know much else about her. I knew she was divorced but other than that, nothing about her personal life."

"Well, now it's up to her to fill in the blanks. Hopefully I can talk to her tonight after work," I hopefully said.

Later on that evening, I made my way to the main bar at *The Cave* and stalked my way up to Rose. "Where's Ryann?" I gritted through my teeth, already knowing she wasn't here.

"I don't know, Nathan. She asked me to leave her alone for a couple of days so she can figure some stuff out. All I can say is I hope your sister can keep her mouth shut," she angrily said. If looks could kill, I would be dead.

"She will," I said, then immediately left. If Ryann wasn't working, there was no point in me staying there. I sent her a text.

Me- Rose told me you turned your phone off. I understand. Let's figure this out together butterfly. Please call me.

I went back to my sister's for the night. If I wasn't going to figure things out with Ryann, I might as well spend the evening enjoying fireworks with my daughter.

Throughout the next couple days, I called and texted Ryann several times to no avail. I had to admit, she was one stubborn woman. I thought about going over to her house and demanding she talk to me. But the last thing I wanted to do was make Ryann feel like I'd backed her into a corner. I didn't want to make her run any further away than she already had.

On Tuesday morning, I got the dreaded break-up text. Was she fucking kidding me? If that was how Ryann thought she would get out of talking to me, she was dead wrong. I sent her a text back letting her know that this was not over. How dare she? And then to send it just hours before she knew I was playing in a tournament. I needed to not let Ryann get in my head. I needed to win the tournament to gain a new online sponsorship.

After the first night, I was doing fairly well. I was tied for fourth place with three other players. A few guys that I know from the tour were going out to one of the bars for drinks and invited me along. Since Ella was having a baking night with her aunt, I figured I was good for a few. Three hours later, a few became a few too many. I could feel the anger I'd been keeping inside over the situation with Ryann rising in me. It made my blood start to boil. Ryann didn't trust me enough to tell me her real job. She didn't have the guts to even call me and explain. All I got was some stupid text. I needed to see her. We needed to figure things out.

Making my way through the lobby of the Bellagio, I headed toward the taxi pick up. I knew I was way too drunk to drive. But I wasn't too drunk to see G quickly rushing inside hotel. He had a hot red-head that he was escorting with him. As they got closer to me, my heart stopped. Butterfly tattoos. *Ryann.* My fucking butterfly was with him. What the fuck? The day she ends it with me she's running off with him. I wanted to stop her, but being as drunk as I was, I didn't think it was a smart idea. Instead, I sent her a pretty bad drunk text.

Me- I see u. wht r u doing wit G? Didt tak u long too mov on.

I needed to get the hell out of there. Grabbing a taxi, I made my way to *The Cave*, hoping Rose would know what the hell was going on. Between what I just saw and the warm night air, I was sobering up real quick.

I walked into Damon's office before I went out to the bar. "Hey, man," I said as I sat down on the couch.

"Bro, you and Ryann need to figure this shit out. First she doesn't show up on the 4th, and now tonight she just fucking disappears. What did you do to her?" he yelled.

"Well she's at the Bellagio with G," I answered coldly. "I saw her with him after I left the bar with a few of my poker buddies. I haven't spoken to her since the 4th either, so I'm just as lost as you are, man. Did you ask Rose what happened?"

"She told me she had no idea what happened."

"Rose is lying. She always knows what's going on with Ryann." I storm out of the office and make my way to the main bar.

"Rose. Break time. Now." I didn't give her a choice but to come with me when I grabbed her arm and dragged her to the back with me.

We make our way out back so that no one else would hear. Neither she nor I needed the problems that could come with all this. "Don't bullshit me, Rose. I'm not Damon. What the hell happened here tonight? And why is Ryann at the Bellagio with G?"

"She's where?" Rose asked, shocked.

"I saw her in the lobby of the Bellagio with G as I was leaving to come here. She was still in her schoolgirl costume. What the hell happened here tonight?"

"Vanessa came up and asked her if she would do a private groom dance for a bachelor party, and being her job, she agreed." I did everything to hold back my scowl. "Then G came to the bar looking for her. I didn't think he found her. Next thing I know, I see Ryann running to the back, and before I could go check on her, Lucas was at my bar."

"Wait. Ex-husband, Lucas? What was he doing here?" Worry starts to take over learning Ryann's ex had been in the club.

"Nathan, he was the groom. Ryann was asked to do a dance for her ex," Rose said trying not to cry.

"Did you try and call her?" I asked.

"Of course I did. Her purse and phone are here so calling her did no good. Since her car and everything was still here, I assumed she had found you. But I guess she found G instead. At least we know she's safe. G would never let anything happen to her."

Knowing Ryann was with G, I didn't like it. He was the one who was there when she needed someone. I should've been there, not at the bar. It should have been my arms that she ran into. But would that have made it worse for her? All I could do was hope that she was smart enough to know who he really was, and to still believe in what we had.

The next morning, I woke up to see that all hell had broken loose on social media. There was a TMZ photographer in the lobby of the Bellagio the night before. The tournament I was playing in had a few celebrity players. Oh, this was not good. The headline read:

NFL Playboy Richard Grovanski's New Stripper Squeeze

There was a full picture of them both. Ryann had a wig and contacts on but her tattoos were completely exposed.

It was early but I called Cristina. "Hey. I have two questions," I said.

"Good morning to you too, dear brother. I may have two answers," she laughed.

"Ryann's ex-husband works for the same school district as her, correct?"

"Yeah at the high school. Why?"

"He was one of Ryann's clients last night."

"Oh, my God."

"Right? It was his bachelor party of all things. Next, how many of the teachers at school know about her butterfly tattoos?"

"Most. Ryann's proud of them," my sister answered.

"Shit. Her problems are much bigger than you

knowing who she is."

"Nathan, what are you talking about?"

"Check out TMZ," I responded before ending the call.

I got to the Bellagio early to see if I could find out which room belonged to G, but of course there was no one there registered to that name. Not surprising.

I'd be tied up in the tournament for the next twelve hours and there wasn't anywhere I wanted to be less. I sent her text before I started playing.

Me- Butterfly- I've seen the news. Do not shut me out. Can we please talk tonight?

I went into the poker room and did my best to concentrate on my game. As much I wanted to go be with Ryann and be her support, I couldn't blow a half-million-dollar online poker deal. By lunch break, I was anxious to check to see if she'd gotten back to me. Pulling out my phone, my shoulders slumped when there was nothing from Ryann, but there was a message from Damon.

Damon- Ryann came by to get her purse and car. She's a mess dude. I gave her a couple days off.

Me- Thanks man.

The rest of the day went by smoothly. I continued to do well in the tournament even though it was the last place I wanted to be. By the time the night was over, I was tied for second with some actor I'd never heard of. I pulled my phone out to call and say goodnight to Ella and noticed a text message.

Ryann- K

Oh, thank fuck. At least I knew I wouldn't get the door slammed in my face. I Facetimed Ella and told her I couldn't wait to get her back to my house tomorrow so she'd better enjoy her last night with Aunt Cristina and Jackson. I jumped on my Harley and raced to Ryann's as quickly as I could ride.

Thirty minutes later, I pulled into Ryann's driveway. When she opened the door I could see her eyes were red and puffy, a dead giveaway that she'd been crying. As soon as she saw me, she threw her arms around my neck and held on for dear life. As I carefully lifted her up, she threw her legs around my waist and I carried her into the living room.

"I'm so sorry, Nathan," she whispered into my neck. She sniffled and started to cry again.

"Shhhh...its okay, butterfly. We'll work this out." But as I said that, I started to wonder what we were working out. Were we working out the fact that she couldn't tell me about her job, or that she broke up with me over text, or that she spent the night with G? Could I forgive her if she had sex with G?

I held her in my arms for a few minutes as she continued to cry. As much as I wanted to know everything, Ryann would tell me when she was ready. The coconut from her hair began to invade my senses. Her scent was so damn intoxicating. I was addicted to this woman. Was it too early to say I was falling in love with her?

"Ryann, we need to talk. Too much has happened in the last few weeks to just sit here and brush things under the rug," I told her.

"I know," she said quietly. "I'm not even sure what to say or where to begin."

"Okay. Well, how about at the beginning." She nodded in agreement.

Over the next hour, Ryann explained to me that she and Lucas were both teachers with almost equal income, so there was no extra support from the divorce. As a result, she found herself struggling financially over the past year, and the only solution was moving home. Until Rose suggested she start dancing.

"I still don't understand why you didn't think you could trust me with this, Ryann," I said bluntly.

"Embarrassment mainly. But also fear. If anyone found out who I was, I'd lose everything. And we're still so new. When I met you, you were the poker player in the background who had a private booth at a strip club. I mean c'mon, Nathan," she said coming off slightly judgmental.

"Touché," I responded.

"And then when I found out that you were Jackson's amazing Uncle Nate and Cristina was your sister, I felt like someone ripped the rug out from underneath me. Everything came crashing down around me. I think your sister is an amazing woman, I do, but that lady can gossip," she continued.

"So why end things with a text? We could have talked about it. Tried to figure it out together." I asked.

"Because I was humiliated. What am I supposed to say when I meet your parents? Why yes I was Jackson's teacher and your son's stripper girlfriend," she blurted out.

I couldn't help but burst out laughing at her. She was so cute when she was frustrated. "Ryann, really?" She just shrugged. "Okay. I don't like it, but I guess I understand. Rose told me what happened with Lucas. Are you alright?"

"No. But I will be I guess. Now that was mortifying. I went running out of the club, ran straight into G and he got me out of there. Nathan, I know you saw me. I got your text and Damon told me. I'm so sorry."

"Ryann, I'm only going to ask you this once, so please tell me the fucking truth. Did you have sex with Richard Grovanski?"

"No, I didn't."

"Why?"

"You Nathan. Us. We're the reason I didn't sleep with Rich."

That was all I needed to hear. My lips landed exactly where they had been dying to be since the moment I walked through her door. That pouting bottom lip had been begging to be kissed. Her mouth opened to mine without hesitation. Our tongues greedily reached out for one another like we were fighting for the last drop of water. Our teeth crashed together as we fought to deepen the kiss that we'd both been craving so deeply.

Reluctantly, I pulled away from her mouth. "Ryann, I

need you to promise that you won't run from me...from us...again. Shit's about to get worse before it gets better, but, butterfly, I will be your rock. I want to be the arms you find when you're scared or upset," I told her gently.

Ryann put her head back on my shoulder. "It's bad isn't it? What the hell was I thinking going to the Bellagio with G?"

"You were thinking you needed to get the hell away from Lucas and a really bad situation. I'm sorry I wasn't there for you. I should have been at the club and not at a bar getting drunk and being pissed off," I said kissing the top of her head.

"Stop, Nathan. I did this. Not you. I broke it off with you. I ran off with G. Now the consequences are mine."

"Ours, butterfly. The consequences are ours." I pulled Ryann up off the couch. "C'mon let's go do something."

"Nathan, it's late and don't you have to finish a tournament tomorrow?" she asked.

"Yeah, but this is something that I need to do." I used the tone of voice that I knew would have Ryann doing whatever I wanted her to do. She got this wicked little smile each time I took control.

I handed Ryann her helmet and we took off on my bike. As we sped out of town, I could feel her tits pressed hard against my back each time I went around a corner. The harder she squeezed the more my dick grew. She noticed that I had to keep adjusting my junk. It was becoming a painful thirty-minute ride.

We pulled up to our rock in the middle of the desert. I knew this was the perfect time and place to do exactly what I'd been dreaming about since the first day I had Ryann on the back of my bike. When I stopped, she climbed off the back, but I stayed right where I was.

"Aren't you getting off?" she asked, slightly puzzled.

I crooked my finger at her. It'd been less than a week since I'd tasted my girl. Less than a week since I'd been inside my beautiful woman. I was craving her like a fat kid craves cake. I wanted to make sure that Ryann knew she was mine and I no longer planned on sharing her with anyone.

I moved my ass to the back seat. "Get on," I told. She moved to climb on like she was going to drive my bike. Hadn't thought of that, but it would be sexy as hell.

"Other way, butterfly. Face me." Embarrassment flooded her face. The pink color she turned when she blushed made her so fucking cute.

She got on my bike facing me, and instantly my lips were on hers. Ryann moved her hands under my t-shirt and ran her nails across my chest. I made quick work of her shirt and tore it off her body. Pushing her bra down to expose her perfectly huge tits, my mouth moved down her chest and found its way to her already erect nipples. I continued to suck, letting out a loud pop every time I let one go.

Getting off the bike, I had Ryann swing her legs over to one side. I pulled her jeans down around her ankles, and moved her sexy little G-string to the side. "You're so sexy naked here in the moonlight, butterfly. I can see how wet you are. You're fucking glistening," I said to her, then slid two fingers in her soaking pussy.

"Nathan, you make me feel so good," she whispered.

"There's no one for miles. Scream my name, baby. I want to hear how good I make you feel," I demanded.

"Mmmm...you're going to have to do more than that to make me scream, nuts," Ryann giggled.

"Oh, is that so?" I asked. I suddenly lifted her off my bike and bent her ass over the seat. Without her expecting it, I gave her a swift smack on her ass.

"Nathan!" she screamed.

"That's more like it. I fucking love when you say my name."

"Nathan, fuck me now, baby."

"Anything you wish, butterfly."

Having Ryann laid out across my bike, with my cock pushing in and out of her sweet pussy was one of the best feelings ever. Her body was beautiful, her tits were amazing and her pussy literally felt like it was made for my dick.

"Cum with me, Nathan. Cum with me, baby," she shouted. With that, I lost myself completely inside of her.

I pulled her up to face me. "That was beautiful, Ryann. But there was something different for me tonight," I told her. I could feel her trying to wiggle out of my hold, something she did whenever she was getting uncomfortable. "Ah, ah, ah! What have I told you about trying to wiggle away from me?"

"Well, different usually isn't a good word," she said with a worried look on her face.

"But, you didn't let me finish. Tonight, for me, wasn't about making me feel good anymore, it was about making you feel good. Ryann, I've fallen for you. Hard. And every day I will fight to make you feel good."

CHAPTER THIRTEEN
RYANN

Harder to Breathe

Holy. Shit. TMZ. This couldn't be happening. When I left with Rich the night before, I left all my things behind. I was so upset from having to dance for Lucas that my only thought was to get the hell out of there. After a few drinks, the thought never crossed mind that anyone would even be wondering where I was. But apparently it wasn't too long until everyone found out where I was anyways. I completely forgot that Nathan's tournament was at the Bellagio. And it fucking figured it would be a celebrity tournament with the paparazzi.

Deciding not to look at my phone until I got home, I hit the Bluetooth in my car to call Rose. She had to keep me from seeing the mess I just made for myself.

"Where the fuck have you been?" she screamed before I could even say hello.

"Well, good morning to you to," I responded.

"Don't even give me that shit. I see you have your phone back. Where are you?"

"Meet me at my house in twenty," I told her.

We both pulled up at the same time. I could see the angry look on her face, but also that look of concern only Rose could give me. Before we even made it through the front door, she pulled me into a hug so tight that I almost couldn't breathe.

"Is it that bad?" I asked.

"You haven't checked it out yet?"

"No. I just got my phone back. Once Damon told me I was on TMZ, I didn't want to look at anything until I got home." I replied.

"C'mon. Let's go inside." *Shit.*

I let Roxy out, cleaned up her mess since she'd been locked for over twelve hours, and let Rose turn on the computer. All I could hope was that my Vaughn get-up disguised me enough that no one could recognize me. My jaw hit the ground when I saw the picture was sprawled all over the internet. Right there in full color were my beautiful butterfly tattoos. My tattoos are something that I'm proud of. I believed that my babies should be remembered and talked about, so I often showed them to people.

I sat there stunned. If things weren't bad before they were sure going to get bad now. Between Lucas and now the pictures, there was no going back to the Ryann I was before. I felt like someone had punched me in the stomach. The tears started to build in my eyes, my hands started to shake, it became hard to breathe. I could feel the anxiety attack coming on.

"Go lay down. Now!" Rose demanded. "Give me your phone."

I did my best to calm down and listen to her. A few minutes later she brought me a Xanax and a bottle of water. Again, she knew me all too well.

"Alright, let's see what we have here," she said as she started scrolling through my phone. "Missed calls from me, your mom, Lucas, and Nathan, and same for the text messages. I'm just going to delete all this social media crap."

"Anything that I need to hear? Nothing from Lucas please. I'll deal with him later. What did Nathan say?"

"He's seen the news and wants to see you tonight."

"K," was all I said.

"Sent," Rose snickered.

"Wait, what?"

"You said "K," so I assumed you wanted to see Nathan."

"No, bitch, I was saying "K" to you. I broke it off with him, remember? I really don't want to deal with all of this right now."

"Too late. You can thank me later," she bluntly told me.

I slept for most of the day. When I woke up, Rose was gone and I had no idea when or if Nathan was coming over because I hadn't heard from him since Rose sent him that text. I knew he was playing in a tournament, but didn't know what time it was over. I decided now was as good of a time as any to start reading my missed messages.

Text messages were first. My mom, Nathan and Rose were all very concerned about me. But Lucas just straight out got hateful.

Lucas- What the fuck Ryann? Great way to tarnish your name and your reputation. I always knew you were a slut.

You've got to be kidding me right? He was the one who left me! He was the one in a strip club already getting married again! What right did he have to call me anything? I couldn't stop the angry tears from falling. Lucas McKennan would get what's coming to him.

When I checked my Facebook most of the messages were from friends or coworkers asking if it was me or that some stripper had the same tattoo as me. I'm glad that not everyone recognized me.

I decided to call my mother back. "Hey, Mom," I said when she finally picked up. I had no idea what time zone she was vacationing in.

"Good morning, sweetie," she muttered, still half asleep.

"Morning?" I asked.

"Yeah, it's three fifteen a.m. here in Paris. It's okay. How are you? Was that you on TMZ?"

I explained to my mother everything that had happened over the last month. "I'm not sure if I'm ashamed that you're a stripper or proud that you are dating a pro football player," was her only response.

"Thanks, Mother," I said sarcastically. "On that note, I'll talk to you later." I curled myself up on the couch and cried.

When the doorbell rang, I wasn't sure if I was scared, relieved, or pissed off. I seemed to have all the emotions immediately rushing through my brain. But as soon as I saw Nathan's eyes looking at me with such genuine care and concern, I jumped into his arms and held on for dear life.

I told Nathan everything. There was no need to hold back anything from him now, and I cared enough about him to give him an honest answer. He took me for the most amazing ride of my life. Being naked across his bike was so exhilarating. In that moment, I realized the true meaning of reckless abandon. With Nathan, I felt free. And when he told me he was falling for me I knew that I would be safe. No matter what happened in the future.

Nathan and I went back to my place to get some sleep before he had to play in the last day of his sponsorship tournament and then he needed to spend some time with Ella. I was off work until Monday, so I figured I would use the time to figure out my next move.

I called my closest friend and teacher union representative, Melinda, to get some advice on what was left of my teaching career.

"Holy shit, Ry, that was you?" she practically yelled into the phone.

"Yeah, it was," I confessed. I explained the entire story to her.

"Wow, lady, that is one hell of a summer vacation," Melinda pointed out. "I had no idea that you were struggling so bad. You always said everything was good."

"Yeah, well, not so much."

"And, wait let me get this straight. The groom you danced for was Lucas?" she asked.

"Yeah, and he has been sending me horrid text messages. He seriously called me a slut. I don't trust him at all."

"Well, to be honest, you have only two choices. You can wait to see what happens and hope you don't get caught. If you do, you risk losing your teaching credential. Or resign before the district forces you to. If you do that, you may get away with your credential since they didn't have to ask you to leave," she told me.

"Thanks, Mel. You've given me a lot to think about."

By Friday morning, I had become extremely pissed off that Rich had not called me to see how I was dealing with all of the media attention. Maybe it was something he was used to, but I sure as hell wasn't. I knew he was at a kid's training camp, but he didn't live under a rock. Should I call him or wait? I mean it really didn't matter at this point because Nathan was my man and I knew that without a doubt. Yet I couldn't help but wonder what happened to that teddy bear of a man that held me the other night.

My thoughts were interrupted by the alert of a text message. God, please don't let it be another one from Lucas.

Nathan - Hi butterfly. I miss you something fierce. Ella and I will be there in 2 hours to get you. Pack for the weekend.

Me - Where are we going?

Nathan - Surprises, baby. I am full of surprises.

Holy crap. I was meeting Nathan's daughter. What if she didn't like me? What if I didn't like her? What if she's jealous? Fuck, what if I'm jealous? All of this was just nonsense. Ella and I were going to get along just fine. I hoped.

Two hours later I heard Nathan's truck pull up in my driveway. My hands started to shake as I opened the door. My nervousness was obvious to Nathan. "Calm down, butterfly. She doesn't bite," he whispered in my ear when he hugged me hello.

"Hi, Ms. McKennan. These are for you," Ella sweetly said to me handing me some beautiful flowers. She quickly ran to the back door as soon as she saw Roxy in the backyard.

"Jackson says he's really mad because I get to meet Roxy before he does." She giggled as she blew my dog kisses through the window.

Nathan came up from behind me and whispered, "We're going to have to do something about that last name of yours, butterfly." He discreetly placed soft kisses on the back of my neck.

Feeling the goosebumps take over my skin, I knew I

needed to change the subject. "Are we taking Roxy to your place again?"

"We sure are. Let's get a move on so we don't miss our flight," Nathan said clapping his hands and shuffling us all out the door.

A few hours later, we pulled up to a private runway at the Las Vegas airport. I was in major shock when I saw what was waiting for us.

"Holy wow, Nathan. A private jet?" I asked.

"Holy wow?" he chuckled back at me.

"Sorry," I smiled. "Good language is a habit around kids."

"I think it's cute," he kissed me on the nose. "Only the best for my girls."

Ella took the seat next to me rather than the seat next to her dad. It made me extremely nervous at first, but then I realized she wanted to work together to try and figure out where we were going. I figured she was in on the surprise with Nathan. But her not knowing gave us something to bond over.

Since we were over land, we quickly determined we were flying east. Ella was an exceptional young lady. From our conversations, I could tell that she was bright, determined, and creative. All the things I would have wanted my daughter to be. As Ella and I continued to bond, I occasionally caught Nathan watching us and smiling. For my life feeling like it was falling apart earlier in the week, this seemed to be the start to a perfect ending.

By the flight times, Ella and I were able to figure out that we were either going to Florida or New York. When the bright lights of the city skyline came into view, I was a giddy little school girl right along with Ella. I loved New York City.

Being a teacher I'd never really lived in the lap of luxury. But after flying on a private jet and making love in a bed at the Four Seasons overlooking the city, a girl could get used to that type of lifestyle.

Nathan definitely put so much thought into the weekend, so the three of us could bond together. Central Park Zoo, Lion King on Broadway, and the Statue of Liberty were all on the agenda. It was crazy to think that the life that I'd always wanted with Lucas, I was now finding it with a man I met working as a stripper.

The barrage of text messages from Lucas kept coming, so I had to turn off my phone for the entire day; calling me a slut and a whore, threatening to tell the school board of my "extra-curricular" activities. Why was he acting that way?

Nathan flashed me a look that told me get out of my head. If he only knew.

When we arrived back at the hotel, late Saturday evening, my body was exhausted from all the walking we'd been doing. Nathan tucked Ella into bed in her room. I could hear the mumblings of a conversation from the other room and as much as the nosy part of me wanted to eavesdrop, I decided it was best not to. I went into the bathroom and drew myself a bath in the deep tub.

I stepped in the hot water, letting the warmth relax every muscle of my aching feet. Sinking down and closing my eyes, I heard Nathan enter our room and undress.

"Honey, are you joining me?" I asked in my sexy, 'you better come here and fuck me' voice.

He didn't answer. I thought I'd said it loud enough for him to hear. I tried again. Still nothing. What was he doing?

"What the hell is this, Ryann?" Nathan stormed in, shoving his phone in my face.

There in front of me were pictures of Rich and I in bed together the night I spent with him. That asshole posted them on the Vaughn Haley Instagram with the caption—*Can't wait to do this again, baby girl. Miss you.*

Oh. Fuck. Me.

I had never seen that look on Nathan's face before. The anger in his eyes was genuine, real, and deep. "You lied to me, Ryann," he raised his voice. "You're in fucking bed with G! I asked you if you slept with him and you said no. I really didn't think you'd lie to me."

My jaw dropped. "I did not lie to you, Nathan. I didn't have sex with G," I told him with complete conviction and honesty.

"It's hard to believe that when I'm seeing this! You're kissing him in this one, Ryann," his voice got louder. "Can't wait to do this again? Right. And I'm just supposed to believe that you didn't have sex with the NFL playboy of the year?"

"Yes, Nathan you are," I did my best to keep my cool

even though I was flaming mad on the inside. "I told you I would never lie to you and I didn't." I started to get myself out of the tub. My relaxing bath was ruined anyway.

"Why am I supposed to believe you? You've lied to me since the day we met," he yelled, sneering at me.

It felt like he punched me in the gut. Never in a million years did I think Nathan would use my omissions against me. I felt the tears start to pool in my eyes. "Because I fucking love you, Nathan," I whispered as I pushed past him and into our room.

Walking over to the window, I stared blankly at the city skyline. I heard the bedroom door shut, then the door to our suite. Nathan walked out and said nothing in response.

I was utterly pissed off at Rich. After the night that I spent with him, I honestly thought he was different from the way the media described him, but the fact that he did this to me on Instagram made me think otherwise. I vaguely remember him snapping a few pictures, but I thought he was just goofing around. And now once again causing problems for Nathan and me.

My first thought was to message Rich and ask him his reasoning for posting the photos when I haven't heard from him since it all went down. But then it hit me that I really didn't care. The only person I cared about walked out the door on me tonight when I admitted to him and myself that I loved him. I had fallen in love with Nathan Sims somewhere in all this mess.

Grabbing my phone, I decided to take of the Rich

problem once and for all. I logged onto the Vaughn Haley Instagram. With one simple press, I deleted the account. Vaughn Haley had caused more headaches in my life this summer than she'd been worth.

I slipped on the sexy, but appropriate nighty I brought and crawled into bed. I was hoping Nathan would have been back by now, but I'd obviously said too much. Hugging his pillow, I cried.

An hour later, I heard the doors shut and Nathan stumbled in. I could smell the alcohol on him. He crawled into bed and put his arm around me. "Butterfly, you awake?" he whispered. I wasn't sure why, but I pretended to be asleep.

"I'm sorry, Ryann. I love you too," he confessed.

The flight home the next afternoon was quiet. We didn't talk about the I love you's exchanged. I wasn't sure if Nathan knew if I was awake or not, but I didn't think that's how either of us planned on saying those words to each other. Ella noticed the silence on the plane, we just explained it as us being tired.

It was after ten by the time Nathan dropped me off at home. "Can I just bring Roxy by in the morning?" he asked.

"Sure," I said, hopping out of the truck. Walking inside my house, I never looked back at Nathan or Ella, because I knew I would start crying.

I slept like shit that night. I tossed and turned, hoping Nathan would show up because technically it was the morning. But he never did. What the hell happened between us?

I woke Monday morning with half a clear head. If nothing else, I knew what I needed to do with my job. I wrote up my resignation letter and sent it to my principal and Human Resources. It killed me to know that I wouldn't get to go back to Rock Canyon with my new group of five year olds. But I knew it was the only chance I had to save my credential and ever teach again.

The First Cut Is the Deepest

With Ella going back to Jordyn's in a couple of weeks, and Ryann having the rest of the week off, I figured that it was the perfect time to take my girls on a weekend getaway. I knew how much they both loved New York so I'd hoped that it would be the perfect trip for them to bond. When we boarded the jet and *my* J-Ella Bean chose the seat next to Ryann instead of me, I knew the surprise trip was perfect for both my girls.

Even though Ryann had been to New York before, she had no problem letting Ella drag her around playing tour guide. The patience that Ryann had with my daughter was amazing. She reacted to everything Ella said like it was the most interesting thing she'd ever heard. I could see from the way Ryann was with her, and the way Jackson talked about her, that she must be amazing with her class. She would make such a wondeful mother.

While Ryann and Ella were in one of the many shops they decided to go in, I scrolled through Facebook and Instagram. I was surprised to see that there were new postings on Ryann's Vaughn Haley page. What the hell? Postings from G. Pictures of Ryann and him in bed together. Holy fuck. They were even kissing in one of them. *Can't wait to do this again.* Really? Ryann fucking lied to me. She did fuck G.

Feeling my blood starting to boil, I didn't know if I was angrier that Ryann had slept with G, or that she lied to me. She'd told me she didn't sleep with G, but I didn't know what to think with these pictures. And why the hell would he post them on social media? My head was fucking spinning. The worst part of it all was I had to wait to say something because I would not make a scene in front of Ella.

The rest of the evening was quiet. When we got back to the hotel, I tucked Ella in bed while Ryann went and started a bath. Once we were in the privacy of our room, I confronted Ryann. The anger in my eyes created such a hurt in hers. Hurt or not, pictures don't lie...people do. My head was all kinds of fucked up.

The last thing I expected in the midst of all this was for her to tell me that she loved me. What the fuck? I knew I should have stayed but I needed to get the hell out of there. Without saying a word, I walked out on her. Leaving her there alone.

I went down to the bar and tried to sort through everything that had happened today. Did I really think she had sex with G? No...yes...I don't know. First shot of whiskey down. I didn't think she'd lie, but it's not like she was completely truthful with me either. Second shot down. My girlfriends' face was out there as the "stripper squeeze" of the most notorious NFL womanizer. Third shot...fuck that one burned. She fucking loved me. Double shot. She said she loved me and I just walked out. I really was a fucking asshole.

As I sat there and scrolled through the pictures over and over again, they suddenly all became unavailable. *What the fuck?* The Vaughn Haley Instagram just disappeared. Gone. Holy shit, Ryann must have deleted it. Was she telling me the truth or was she just trying to hide the evidence of what she did? But the fact that the pictures were with Richard Grovanski meant that they would always be out there. I had two choices here. One: believe Ryann and get over all of this or two: walk away.

I stumbled my way back up to our room and crawled in bed. Pulling her in tight, I told her I was sorry and that I loved her. She pretended to be asleep; she had the cutest little snore when she slept so I knew she was awake. I knew she heard everything I said. For now I'll just let it go. I didn't want Ryann to think the only reason I said this was because I was drunk.

The flight back to Vegas was awkward and quiet. We both knew what we said to one another. But she was hurting and I was drunk. I knew that's not how either one of us planned on sharing those feelings for the first time.

When I dropped her off at home, Ryann could barely look at me. And worse, she said virtually nothing to Ella. I told her I would bring Roxy back in the morning. As soon as I got home, I wanted to take Roxy right over to her. But I wasn't ready to talk to her yet.

On Monday morning, Cristina came back to drop off some things that Ella had left at her house. I told her about everything that happened in New York.

"Nathan, do you really love her or was it the whiskey talking? Ryann has been through so much in the last few years and the last thing she needs is you adding to that," Cristina lectured me.

"I do...at least I think I do. But these pictures are hard to deny," I admitted.

"Okay, I understand that. But to quote one of the best TV lines of all time—'You were on a break!'" Cristina shouted.

"Really?" I glared at her with my best evil eyes.

"So if you can't take Ryann for her word, then there's only one other way to find out. Ask the football guy. You say he's at the club all the time. So straight up ask him." Honestly, I didn't know why I hadn't thought of that before.

At that same moment, Roxy came charging in and started to lick Cristina's feet. I about died laughing watching her freak out at the toe licking pit bull. "What the fudge?" she screamed. That made me laugh even harder. But it also reminded me that I still had Ryann's dog. I needed to take Roxy back, but I still wanted to get my head on straight.

"Huge favor, sis. Will you please take Roxy back to Ryann this morning? I really want to say and do the right thing here and I don't think I can do that if I'm alone with her."

"Really? Okay. I'm not going to question you, but figure this out, Nathan, for both your sakes," she said, sounding disappointed.

I spent the rest of the day trying to figure out what to

do next. I loved Ryann, and now even though it was in the midst of a fight, I knew she loved me too. I knew I didn't want to walk away, but the hurt ran deep. I knew that she spent the night with G, but she told me she didn't have sex with him. But those damn pictures; Ryann was in his bed, in his shirt, kissing his mouth. Break or not, it pissed me off. I understood she needed someone that night after the ordeal with Lucas...but fuck!

I hated that I was avoiding Ryann. There was no other way to admit it except that I was scared as fuck. I wasn't sure what would happen if I found out she was lying to me. Would I be able to forgive her? But worse, what if she was telling me the truth. Would she ever be able to forgive me?

I went to the club on Tuesday night to talk to Rose. I knew it should be Ryann that I was talking to, but for some reason I was more willing to try to get something out of her best friend. Figuring it was her night off, I was surprised to see Ryann's Challenger in the parking lot. I could hear her voice as I made my way to Damon's office. As I drew closer, I couldn't help but eavesdrop.

"Damon, I resigned from my teaching job yesterday. With all the pictures of me on the internet, I took the precaution of quitting before they could fire me. But now I don't have a job. Is it possible that I could stay on? At least until I find something else?" Ryann asked.

"Of course, Ryann. You have a place here as long as you need it. But how does Nathan feel about all of this?" Damon asked her.

"He doesn't know. He hasn't spoken to me since he saw the pictures on that Instagram page Rose made me," she explained. I could hear the hurt in her voice.

"Don't waste your time on that asshat! You know I'm single right?" Damon laughed.

"On that note, I'm gonna go talk to Rose," she laughed with him as she got up and walked out. I darted into one of the hallways so she didn't see me.

As soon as she was out of the back room, I made my way into Damon's office. "So how much of that did you hear?" he asked me.

"More than I needed to. Dude, you're single?"

"Fucker, I saw you come in on the security monitor. I knew you were listening the entire time. But, man, that girl is hurting and you need to fix it," Damon told me. Damn, I'm getting lectured by everybody.

"I know. I'm working on it. I came here to talk to Rose, and instead found Ryann talking to you."

"Why Rose? Why not Ryann?" he asked.

"Because I'm fucking scared of what she's going to say to me. I don't want to lose her, Damon."

"Well, then you better get your ass out to the bar," he warned as he rotated the security monitor to face me. At the bar G was sitting with Ryann, his hand on her knee. Instant anger rushed through my entire body. I practically threw the chair as I stood up to confront them both.

"Don't do anything stupid, nuts," Damon called after me as I stormed out of his office.

Feeling like I'd made it across the club in record time, I knew Damon was behind me. He alerted Ryann and G. Charging toward them, I saw the expressions on their faces change when I approached them. If Ryann was trying to hide something this was not the place to do it.

"Nathan, what are you doing here?" Ryann asked.

"I'd ask you that same question, but obviously I know the answer," I snidely remarked gesturing to the hand still resting on her knee.

"Whatever. I came here to talk to Rose, and Rich happened to be on the other side of the bar asking how to get ahold of me since the Vaughn Haley page was the *only* contact he had for me," Ryann yelled. Shit, was that true? Ryann hadn't given him any contact information.

"Oh, it's Rich now, huh?" I quipped. What the fuck was that? I was just too pissed off in that moment to say anything else.

Rose rolled her eyes. "Yes, this is Rich. You're Nathan, and she's Ryann. Will the three of you go figure this shit out and leave me the hell out of it!" she yelled at us.

Ryann jumped off the bar stool and grabbed my hand. "Come on. Let's walk out back," she said. She nodded at Rich to follow us.

Silently, the three of us walked through the backroom and into the parking lot. I lowered the tailgate on my truck giving Ryann and I a place to sit, which left Rich standing there staring at us both.

"Rich, please tell Nathan that nothing happened between us that night," Ryann began.

"Ryann, I can't do that. That's what I was trying to tell you inside before we were interrupted," Rich said looking directly at her. "Something did happen that night. For me anyways." What the hell was this guy saying?

"What?" Ryann blurted out.

"I started to feel something for you that night. The fact that you wouldn't have sex with me just because I play in the NFL was such a turn on. And I respected you so much more for that," Rich told her. Did this porchdick forget I was here?

"Rich, it had nothing to do with you being a football player or not. I didn't sleep with you because I am in love with Nathan. Split up that night or not, I wasn't going to do that to him," Ryann explained. Now I felt like the porchdick.

Ryann turned and looked at me. "Nathan, that night I needed comforting. Rich was there. We kissed. That's it. Lonely, mad, drunk, confused...no excuse. But I told you the truth." She turned to Rich and asked, "Why did you post the pictures of us in bed?"

"Because it was the only way to find you," Rich answered. "Ryann, I will respect you and Nathan. I'm not the kind of guy to get in the middle of something. But remember, I'm always here for you, baby girl." With that, Rich shook my hand, hugged Ryann, turned around and walked off.

Turning my body to face her, I could see the tears running down Ryann's cheeks. I gently cupped her face, and brushed the tears away. "Please don't cry, beautiful. I'm so sorry I didn't trust in you. In us."

"I told you, Nathan that I wouldn't lie to you," Ryann continued to cry. "And then you fucking send your sister to bring my dog home!"

"I was scared, Ryann. Nothing about this situation is familiar to me. I love you so much. It would have devastated me to be right. And knowing now that I was wrong, I'm terrified that you'll never forgive me." She crawled up into my lap and threw her arms around my neck. Please let her forgive me.

"I'm scared too," she whispered.

"Why did you resign from teaching? You know I have enough money to make those pictures go away," I told her. I hated flaunting my money, but I'd do anything to protect those I love.

"It's not about the pictures anymore. If the pictures don't out me, Lucas will." She pulled out her cell phone and showed me all the text messages from Lucas over the weekend. "If I resigned before he could take any of this to the school board then I might save my teaching credential."

My fists clenched tighter and tighter as I read through the messages Lucas had been sending her. How dare he say any of those things to her? I was going to make sure the asshole got what's coming to him.

"Nathan, stop. This is on me, not him," Ryann told me. I didn't care what she said, I would protect what was mine. "Nathan, just take me home please," she requested.

"My house or your house?" I asked her.

"It doesn't matter. Home is where you are," Ryann beamed as she held on to me tighter.

The next morning, I awoke to that damn dog licking my toes again. Ryann was already outside drinking her morning coffee on the patio, reading something on her Kindle again. Those book boyfriends set some pretty high expectations for guys.

Walking up behind her, I kissed the top of her head. "Good morning, beautiful."

"Mmmm...good morning, handsome," she moaned back. "Coffee's on the counter."

"Last night was hella crazy, huh?" Ryann asked as I sat down at the patio table with her.

"Yeah, just a little," narrowing my eyes at my hated word.

"Wanna talk about it?" she asked me.

"Ryann, do you really want to work at *The Cave* full time?"

"Of course not, Nathan, but what other choice do I have?"

"Move in with me," I boldly stated.

"What?" she asked, shocked by the question.

I grabbed Ryann's hand and pulled her into my lap. "Butterfly, you are mine. I want you to be my girlfriend until you're ready to be my wife. I don't want to share you with other guys at the club anymore. I know you're an independent woman, but let me take care of you until all of this is figured out. Do this for me, please," I was almost begging her.

"Yes," was the only word she said and the only word I needed to hear. I cupped Ryann's face in my hands and kissed those pouty lips that had been calling my name all morning.

"If you could do anything in this world, what would you want to do?" I asked her.

"Honestly, be a mother, Nathan."

"Then let's make that happen."

EPILOGUE
RYANN

One Year Later

 I watched my husband splash around in the pool with our twins and my step-daughter. Never in a million years did I picture my life where it is today. Last summer my life was falling apart around me, and now I saw all my dreams coming true in front of me. Nathan and I married six months ago. It may have seemed quick, but when you know it's the real thing, why wait? When Nathan told me he would make me a mother I wasn't sure what to expect. The possibility of having another miscarriage scared the hell out of me. My heart filled with so much love when he started talking about adoption. And when the agency told us about the twins, we knew our family would be complete.

 After moving in with Nathan, I quit working at *The Cave.* But I did some of the group and feature dances on the weekend, because I enjoyed it. However, Nathan insisted that there were no more lap dances for anyone but him. I actually took a job working at Ms. Jewel's Dance Studio a few nights a week, teaching pole dancing classes. Nathan told me I didn't have to work, but I wanted to keep some of my independence. I depended on Lucas too much and would never put myself in that position again.

 Even though I repeatedly told Nathan to leave the

situation with Lucas alone, he didn't. He kept saying something about needing to protect those that he loved. I tried explaining to him that Lucas couldn't hurt me anymore. Despite having to leave a job I loved, I knew better things were in my future. But Nathan was insistent. Lucas was marrying one of his seniors from the previous year. She was nineteen, but still not okay. To him the only thing important was making babies, and she was ready to do that for him. What I didn't know was that Lucas was set to inherit a large sum of money upon the birth of his first child. We'd always lived a pretty modest life, so I had no idea that his grandmother was filthy rich; the will stated that the child must be Lucas's biological child.

One Saturday afternoon, Rose and I noticed Mrs. McKennan sitting across from us while out having lunch. I kept noticing her flashing me the dirtiest looks. For the life of me, I had no idea what I had done to have her treat me this way, but I was sure as hell going to find out.

I excused myself from Rose before she could stop me and calmly walked over and confronted Lucas's mother. "Can I ask you why you keep giving me all these horrible looks from across the room?"

"How dare you? After what you did to Lucas. Walking out on him like that," she huffed at me.

"You're not serious, are you, LuAnn? I didn't walk out on Lucas. After the doctors told me I couldn't have children, he walked out on me. What were his words? Oh yes, he changed his mind."

A shocked LuAnn McKennan asked me to sit with her. I explained to her what had happened and the reasons Lucas gave when he suddenly served me with divorce papers. Apparently, the lie he had told everyone was that I was cheating on him. Lucas was never supposed to know about the inheritance, but he accidently overheard his aunt and mother speaking about it one day. And from that moment, LuAnn said the only thing that mattered to Lucas was finding the perfect mother for his children.

What Lucas didn't know was that LuAnn was sole executor to her mother's will, and with that she was granted the ability to redistribute the money as she saw fit. She said she'd been looking for any reason to not give the money to Lucas and his nineteen-year-old bride, who was apparently already pregnant. After finding out what Lucas had done to me, LuAnn decided to divide the half million dollars that was set aside for Lucas's family to all of his cousins. She apologized profusely for what her son did, but I knew I couldn't hold that against her. She wished me luck and told me we should have lunch some time and that she will always think of me as a daughter.

I left her table doing a silent, little happy dance inside. I never wanted to wish ill will on anyone, but Lucas sure as hell had that coming.

Not long after, Nathan and I were married in front of our friends and family on a private estate in Hawaii. That night, I thought my life would never be more prefect. Until the day the agency presented us with a unique situation. They had a set of three-year-old twins, a boy and girl. Their mother had died shortly after they were born, and the father was sick and could no longer care for his children. The agency was looking for someone to take the children together as soon as possible. Nathan and I were there the next day.

"Hello! Earth to Ryann! Are you somewhere in there?" Rose shouted as she pretty much pushed me off my chair.

"Hey! Watch it," I laughed with her. "Sorry. Lost in thought. Looking at my beautiful family."

"You know, I'm still waiting on my thank you," she said sarcastically.

"For what?" I asked.

"Really? If it wasn't for me convincing you to work at *The Cave* then you would be living back in California with your mother and her nudist boyfriend." I cringed at her comment. "Instead you have fallen into this beautiful life with your three adorable children." Ella decided to come and live with us for a year while Jordyn spent some time traveling with her new husband. Ella didn't talk very highly of him.

"Well, thank you, Rose. You're my best friend and each day I'm grateful for the life you have given me. I would have never found true happiness without you. There. Good enough?" I smiled at her.

"Sarcastic bitch," she said as she tried to give me a dirty look without laughing.

Turning our attention back to the pool, we saw Jeremy do a cannonball into the water, right in front of us. We tried to be pissed off at him, but the cool water felt too good on our sweaty bodies. Neither one of us could turn away from watching our husbands playing with our kids. The smiles and the laughter coming from our two men was sexy. Watching Jeremy toss around Ali and Ella, had me ogling just a bit. His arms were huge. As I glanced over, I saw Rose watching Nathan play with the twins. Hmmm...this could be interesting.

"Damn we're some lucky girls, aren't we, Ryann?"

"Yes, we are, Rose. Yes, we are."

THE END

Reckless Behavior

Prologue
Rose

5 years ago

"You ready sweets?" Jeremy asks as we drive up to Amouret'te.

"Not going to lie, I am nervous. But I am so fucking ready to see everything that Travis and Ari told us about. Are they still supposed to be meeting us here?"

"They're already here."

As my husband walks around his truck to help me down (being the southern gentleman that he is, I am *never* allowed to open my own door), I take my last deep breath.

With each step we take, I grip Jeremy's hand a bit harder. "Rose, we only do what you are comfortable with. We stop when you say stop."

Thank you. I'm good."

Jeremy guides us directly to the main bar where we meet up with our friends. In a previous conversation, we decided a tour of Amouret'te would be best if we split up.

227

Even though Travis and his wife Ari have only been in Las Vegas six months, we've known them since high school back in Santa Cruz. Travis and I briefly dated before Jeremy moved to California from Nashville, but we were more fun than serious.

"You ready sexy?" Travis asks me, taking my hand and pulling me away from my husband and his wife.

"Yeah," I shyly respond.

"Once you get over the nervousness and let yourself go, swinging can be an amazing experience."

I nod. A few weeks ago, while out for drinks, Ari let it slip that her and Travis were looking for a new swingers' club since moving here to Vegas. Needless to say, Jeremy and I were shocked, and intrigued. It's something that we have talked about but weren't sure how to get into.

Travis never let go of my hand as we walk through the various rooms. There is a room for any "type" of swinging you are into. Yeah, I had no idea that there were so many levels to being a swinger, but there are. There's much more to it than swapping partners.

"This room is for people who like to be watched. Let's go in," Travis explains to me. In the middle of the room is a gorgeously large circular bed, covered in flowing silk sheets. There are bench seats lining all of the walls for the voyeurs. Travis finds a dark corner for us and pulls me down on his lap. Instantly my body tenses. No other man besides my husband has touched me in over 8 years. "Relax, Rose. Jeremy explained your rules to me before we got here. He also told me to get you warmed up for the private room we reserved for later. And besides, it's not like I've never touched you before." I slowly started to breathe again, and let my body relax into his.

"Watch them Rose," he demands as he pushes my face to watch the group in front of us. Two woman and one man were involved in one extremely hot tangled mess of limbs. A young, blonde woman with the most perfect round tits lays flat on her back with her legs pushed back behind her head while a middle aged man pounds his cock in her glistening wet pussy. The other older woman, with bright purple hair and significantly smaller tits, has carefully positioned herself on the face of the blonde. Their hands exploring every inch of each other's bodies.

I can feel the wetness start to form between my legs. "Oh. My. God. This is fucking hot," I whisper. I feel Travis' hands begin to run up and down legs. Goosebumps form on my skin. We continue to watch as the threesome changes positions.

"Let's move on," Travis suggests. He carefully lifts me up and places me back on my feet, grabs my hand and leads me out of the room.

As we're walking through the hallway, Travis grabs both my arms and pushes me up against the wall, his body practically grinding against mine. "You are still so beautiful, Rose. Last time I touched this body, we were just kids. Tell me, sexy, now that you are all grown up, tell me what you like?" he growls in to my neck.

My eyes stare directly into his. Travis is not someone who I am shy about my sexuality with. He is someone I know will always keep me safe. "I like to be spanked."

"I was hoping you'd say that," he whispered upon my lips. I lean in and kiss him. Hard. I know that he has been waiting for me to make the first move, making sure I am comfortable with this situation.

Going to a swingers' club is something that Jeremy and I have been discussing long before we knew our friends were into this lifestyle. It's something we have both fantasized about for years, but were always hesitant for one reason or another; we were too new in our marriage, we were too young, fears of someone different. But after eight years together, the birth of our only child, and finding amazing people that we trust, we knew that this was the right time.

Amouret'te is brand new swingers club in Las Vegas and is already developing an excellent reputation. Our daughter, Ali, is spending the night with my best friend Ryann and her husband Lucas. Travis and Ari are the perfect couple to be with. So Jeremy and I figured why the hell not. And here we are.

Immediately entering the next room, my eyes go wide and my palms start to sweat out of both nervousness and excitement. The walls are lined with all types of spanking devices; leather crops, suede floggers, wooden paddles. My nipples get hard and my pussy starts to drip again as I ache for any of the toys to smack my ass.

The sounds of screams around me quickly breaks me

out of my trance to realize that we are not alone in this room. There are about ten mattresses laid out across the floor with numerous couples or groups involved in some awesome spanking activities.

"Go pick your pleasure," Travis says. "I've been waiting for this."

I walk over to the wall and chose the bright red suede flogger and meet Travis on one the beds. "Get down on all fours, ass towards me, and push up that dress so I can see that smooth, pink ass." I do as he tells me.

His hand gently rubs my ass, preparing it for what's to come. Before I knew it, his hand made swift contact with my cheek. I let out a small yelp. "Oh I need to hear more than that from you Rose." The flogger makes a stinging contact with my flesh.

"FUUUUUCCK!" I yell out catching myself and everyone else in the room off guard.

"That's my girl," Travis roars. "Turn over and lay on your back."

I do as I'm told. Travis lightly runs the edges of the flogger's suede straps up and down the inside of my leg. Fuck this feels so good. My entire body is tingling with delight. He leans his body on top of mine and starts to bite my tits through the thin material of my dress. It makes me so much more comfortable knowing that Travis and Jeremy discussed our rules beforehand so I wouldn't have to be put in the uncomfortable position of having to stop something if it went too far.

Jeremy and I agreed we would only be alone with other partners when we went to clubs with others and ONLY for foreplay. There would be no penetration, of any kind, unless we were together.

Travis pushes himself up and straddles my legs. He takes the flogger and snaps it across my tits. I didn't imagine this to feel so fucking exhilarating. He drags his fingers along the lace of my panties. "Your panties are soaked. I think it's time to find our way to the private room."

I stand up, straightening out my dress. Travis leads me out of the room and down another hallway to a row of private rooms. He unlocks and opens the door. The first thing I lay my eyes on is my husband sitting naked, in all of his glory, his hand in a fist running up and down his large and extremely hard cock. He had been watching a naked Ari dancing on the pole.

"Fuck, sweets, I am so happy to see you," Jeremy said getting up and lifting me into his arms, I wrap my legs around his waist.

"Did you not have a good time with Ari?" I asked.

"I did, but nothing feels the same without you next to me," he whispered into my neck. "Go dance with Ari for me."

I slide off his body, reach down and pull my dress off my body, leaving me standing there in just my panties and heels. Jeremy knows that I have always been turned on by women, so this is as exciting for me as it is for him. I've never danced on a pole before, and Ari sensed my cluelessness. She came up behind me, laced our hands together, and pulled my body into hers. Our bodies melded together and moved to the sound of the music. Feeling her erect nipples pressing into my back was creating such a tingling sensation throughout my entire body. I move my hand down to my sensitive clit, a firm grip grabs wrist to stop me.

"That's my job. I have been waiting all night to touch you," Travis says to me.

Never letting go, Travis pulls me to the bed. He looks back at Jeremy and nods. Before I even realize what is happening, Travis had me on my back with my legs spread. Both he and my husband have a shit-eating grin plastered across their face like they're two kids in a candy store. Travis gives me what I've been wanting. He glides two fingers into my soaking pussy, moving them slowly in and out, bringing me to the release I have been waiting for all night.

I lock eyes with Jeremy, honestly terrified of what I might see looking back at me. Both of our biggest fear is the jealousy that may arise from watching the other with someone else. But all I see in his eyes is lust. And not lust for the woman who is currently sucking his cock, which is quite hot I might add, but lust for me. The same lust he has for me every time he makes love to me alone in our bedroom or when he simply kisses me good morning. Yet something about this is way fucking hotter.

Writing this book was one of the scariest and most rewarding things I have ever done. I could not have done it without the love and support of my friends and family.

Kevin- Thank you for all the love and support you have given me through this process. Your patience means everything. I love you.

Marie and Melina- My two best friends in the world. Your encouragement made me brave enough to embark on this crazy journey. Thank you for always being in my corner. You both were the perfect muses for my characters!

Tiffany J. West- GIRL, I can't say enough! Without you I would have been lost. You have been the best friend and mentor that I could have asked for. Your guidance has been my lifesaver. Tiff's Teasers took my words and made them come to life. Thank you to the moon and back! I think it's time for another mai tai!

Cassia Brightmore- You have been with me from the beginning. From taking this gorgeous photo, editing my words, and promoting me like crazy. I am so glad that we have got to work together and become friends.

T.H. Snyder- You were one for the first people to bring me into this crazy indie author world and I couldn't thank you more. You have been an inspiration. I am so happy to be able to call you a friend.

Lance Jones and Jess Epps- I am so honored to have you both on the cover of my first book. The chemistry in the picture is undeniably hot. From the first time I saw that photo, I knew that you would be the perfect faces for Nathan and Ryann. Your support has been amazing. Thank you both so much.

Kari Ayasha (Cover to Cover Designs) - The cover you created captured the perfect emotion for my characters and book. It was absolutely beautiful. Thank you for all the work you put into it.

Christina Gragg- You took my words and made them "pop". You are an awesome blurb writing!! Thanks!

To all my friends and family- Thank you all so much for your love and support. Having you all by my side means so much to me.

40456425R00137

Made in the USA
San Bernardino, CA
21 October 2016